The Contrary

Thornton Cline

BLACK ROSE
writing™

© 2015 by Thornton Cline

All rights reserved. No part of this book may be reproduced, stored in a retrieval system or transmitted in any form or by any means without the prior written permission of the publishers, except by a reviewer who may quote brief passages in a review to be printed in a newspaper, magazine or journal.

The final approval for this literary material is granted by the author.

First printing

This is a work of fiction. Names, characters, businesses, places, events and incidents are either the products of the author's imagination or used in a fictitious manner. Any resemblance to actual persons, living or dead, or actual events is purely coincidental.

ISBN: 978-1-61296-562-8
PUBLISHED BY BLACK ROSE WRITING
www.blackrosewriting.com

Printed in the United States of America
Suggested retail price $16.95

The Contrary is printed in Book Antiqua

Dedicated to Mom and Dad for always believing and encouraging me.

The Contrary

CHAPTER ONE

THANKSGIVING DAY, 2009 11:52 A.M.

I am sick and tired of all of the gullible and foolish people in this world—nothing but morons. All they do is take up space. I used to angrily complain to myself as I shook my head disapprovingly.

Back then I was a mean-spirited, judgmental and opinionated man. I believed that 95% of the world was full of *idiots* and *gullible, foolish* people. I had no use for *those kinds* and really didn't give a damn about them. I was the kind of person who forced his opinions and beliefs on others and made them feel uncomfortable.

I wasn't always that way. Four years ago, Thanksgiving Day I lost the love of my life Samantha to a long battle with cancer. It took the wind and soul out of me. Samantha was the best friend I ever had. We had been married for 45 years and were a close couple even in high school. We were voted king and queen of our senior prom. Samantha had a pure, genuine and loving heart. Her sincerity was always reflected in her lovely, shining smile. She was strikingly beautiful with her long red hair and

The Contrary

piercing emerald eyes. Samantha made me smile, laugh, cry and feel worthy of her respect. If there was anyone who came close to loving unconditionally it was my dear Samantha. I was so taken with Samantha that I was always there, right beside her in everything we did in life. We were an amazing team. It wasn't fair that Samantha had to suffer like she did from those cruel, vicious tumors. It wasn't acceptable that cancer robbed me of the rest of the time I had with Samantha on Earth.

I was still angry and resentful for having lost the love of my life. Flashbacks of her final days were cruel reminders of how she had wasted away to nothing. She stopped eating and her beautiful angelic body had wasted away until there was nothing left but skin attached to her frail bones.

The day before she went to be with Jesus she managed, somehow as weak as she was, to write her final words to me in a letter. I cherish her letter and hold it close to my heart. I carry it with me everywhere I go. There are many days her words are too painful to read.

In case you are wondering who I am, my name is Louis Green, a retired factory foreman from the small town of Griswold, Iowa. I shamefully confess that I was at one time that mean, despicable, and judgmental man. After Samantha went to be with Jesus, I lived a sad and solitary life. My heart was hardened. I rarely had anyone to talk to except when I called my son and my daughter-in-law. They always found excuses for not talking to me. I was a lifelong Methodist and attended church regularly. But I never developed any close relationships with my so-called *church friends* or any friends for that matter. It was if they were looking right through me as if I didn't exist. But you can't blame them. I was often quick to judge and harshly critical. I always thought that I knew the truth about life and this world. I thought I was perfect. I was narrow-minded in the fact that I thought everyone else was wrong. I had no patience for *gullible and foolish* people. I felt like my opinion was the only one that counted.

I am about to share with you those painful, harsh and dark days when I was that man whom I am not proud to say I was. A series of catastrophic events culminated into one life-threatening day where I was held hostage at gunpoint—a day of living hell. I was supernaturally transformed from that day forward into someone everyone loved to be with. They even honored me with the label, "America's Hero" for an event that happened when I was held hostage.

As I think back to that 2009 Thanksgiving Day I remember a painful, horrific and vivid scene. On my 60-minute drive to visit my son and daughter-in-law in Omaha, Nebraska for Thanksgiving dinner something alarming and strange caught my eyes. Up ahead on that windy two-lane highway about a mile from their home my eyes opened wide. I gasped for breath. I thought I was seeing things. There appeared to be a body lying in the middle of the road. I quickly slammed on my brakes, swerved and skidded 20 yards to a sudden stop. I bolted out of my truck badly shaken, panic-stricken and stood paralyzed with fear in the middle of Cedar Island Road. I stared helplessly at what appeared to be a young girl lying only a few feet from where I stopped my truck. Here I was in a strange town and this was happening.

Oh my God, my God. Think fast Louis. Is she still breathing? Is she still alive? I shouted loudly at myself as fear continued to grip my body. Terror struck my face. I could feel cold shivers all over. I bent down slowly to turn her body.

No, no dear God how could this be? I cried in anguish as I shook my head in disbelief.

I recognized the face of the young girl lying in the road. It

The Contrary

was painful enough to see a girl lying lifelessly in the road but the torment was magnified a hundred times when I realized it was someone dear to me.

It was 11:52 a.m. Thanksgiving Day. Four hours earlier I would have never dreamed in my worst nightmare of anything like this tragedy happening to me.

CHAPTER TWO

FOUR HOURS EARLIER

It wasn't just any cold November day in 2009. Thanksgiving Day had arrived. The pale gray sky stretched as far as anyone could see over the endless golden cornfields of my small town of Griswold, Iowa. I woke myself from my snoring and hurried out of bed. I reached for my glasses and placed them carefully over my ears and nose. The clock by my bed flashed 7:50 a.m. I stretched my arms and legs and took a long, deep yawn. I rushed to take my morning shower, shave, and get dressed. I put on my favorite white oxford shirt and medium blue wool sweater. The wool and cotton felt soft and reminded me of the days when my mother used to hold me close in her arms. Today I decided to wear dress khaki pants instead of regular attire of blue jeans. I forced myself to walk down the stairs and into the kitchen as if I were sleepwalking. I microwaved an egg and bacon biscuit. A burnt, foul odor awakened my senses as I opened the microwave door.

Damn eggs, damn bacon. What a stupid microwave. I cursed as I opened the microwave door.

Normally, most mornings I would crawl out of bed in slow

motion and take my sweet time in making breakfast. I had been retired from the factory for about three years. I had no place to be at any particular time. Many of my days were filled with fly fishing and hunting. I was an active member of the National Rifle Association and loved the great outdoors. I read every book and magazine on the subjects, and I considered myself an expert.

Today, four years ago, Thanksgiving Day was the day I lost the love of my life Samantha to a long battle of cancer. I still felt angry and bitter at the world and at God for her agonizing, painful death. Sometimes the pain was too much to bear.

Before Samantha went to be with Jesus in heaven, I had hundreds of friends on my Facebook page. I would keep my *friends* updated with the latest photographs of what my wife, grandchildren, and I were doing. But after Samantha left this Earth, I began posting mean-spirited, ugly, and opinionated remarks about everything I believed was wrong with the world, especially about politics and religion. I became rude and obnoxious, forcing my opinions on others. Most of my so-called friends unfriended me.

I brushed their actions off: *stupid friends, who needs them anyway*. Some would call me self-righteous because I thought I had the answers to all the world's problems. I now despised the world in general and all of its problems. After I had lost all my Facebook friends, I continued to be outspoken and tell everyone how I felt about the world. I wrote angry letters to editors of newspapers. I posted arrogant, obnoxious, and inflammatory remarks on political blogs. I dreamed of living in a *perfect world* where there were no problems—where only *smart and intelligent people* lived.

Some people would refer to that kind of world as a utopia, but others would call it a bubble.

There are too many gullible and foolish people in this world— nothing but morons. I shook my head with contempt. All of those *uneducated* and *ignorant* people made me unhappy and furious. I had a mission to accomplish. I set out to *educate* the world by being vocal and by joining groups that supported my extreme views.

I believed that 95% of the world couldn't think for themselves. I believed that they were merely *puppets* who followed what the biased left-wing news media told them. I subscribed to the idea that people voted for whomever the news media told them to. I believed that people *bought into* whatever they were told to believe.

But I tried to put all that aside today. I was especially excited. I would be traveling to my son Norris and daughter-in-law Julie's house in Omaha, Nebraska, to see my family: grandchildren, uncles, aunts, nephews, nieces, and cousins. They had planned a Thanksgiving feast and celebration in Norris's 20-room mansion. Many of my family were traveling from distant places to be at this celebration.

God I miss my family.

I was lonely. I hadn't seen my family in years. While I missed most of them, there were a few whom I wanted to forget about because I couldn't get along with them.

Everyone attending this Thanksgiving dinner was expected to bring a covered dish, preferably home-cooked. I figured I would stop to pick up a squash casserole at a supermarket along the 60-minute drive. I led a simple life since I lost my dear Samantha. I rarely cooked anything. I had relied too heavily on Samantha. She was the best cook in the world, making dishes that everyone would beg for: fried catfish, barbecue pork ribs, ravioli, and lasagna. I could simply close my eyes and remember the taste of my favorite dishes. Samantha poured every ounce of her love into making her great dishes, and you could taste her love with every bite.

I took my last gulp of plain black coffee, finished reading the headlines of the *Griswold American* and strutted out the door to

The Contrary

my faithful blue Ford F-150 truck. It was still shiny and new like the day I bought it 12 years ago. I turned the key. The engine roared, and I drove down the old dirt driveway from my rustic farmhouse to the main road. I left behind a long trail of dust that filled the air. As I drove through Griswold to route 92 toward Omaha, I passed the old water tower marked GRISWOLD. I passed the factory that I had worked in as plant manager for a little over 45 years.

It's a shame that they had to shut down the factory and send all of the work to those damn Chinese. I lamented while shaking my head.

I still couldn't get over the fact that many products were not being made in the *great United States of America.*

Damn Congress and those Presidents, I protested heatedly.

If it weren't for that Free Trade Agreement, we'd still have jobs here in this country. I had no problem placing blame.

To me, the signing of that agreement was an act of betrayal to the American workers. It was basically a license to replace them for *cheap labor*. I was still angry about the way a lot of American workers had been eliminated.

I believed that products made in China or other countries were inferior. I believed that they were cheaply made and would not last. And I still resented how my company gave pink slips to my fellow workers; now nearly half of the town was out of work.

To me, farming out work to another country was *un-American*. I felt lucky that I had reached retirement when the factory shut down. I could now collect my Social Security check without having to worry.

Nevertheless, I was proud of my little town of 1,000 people. It was a great place to live. The people were friendly, church-going, flag-saluting folk who always put their families first. Taxes and the cost of living were low. The people seldom littered and kept their town clean and attractive.

I had so many fond memories of Griswold and its people. I was proud that my town was named after a famous Railroad director, J. N. A. Griswold. I often bragged to people that the famous actor Neville Brand was from Griswold. Neville had starred in many television and theatrical films, including ones with Elvis Presley.

I turned onto highway 92 and headed west toward Omaha. Omaha was a large city compared to my town of Griswold. It had skyscrapers, sports teams, hospitals, parks, malls, and colleges—everything one could imagine, including crime. Omaha was the home of Fred Astaire, Mutual of Omaha, and Berkshire Hathaway and was named after the Omaha Indian tribe. I preferred to call them *Indians* instead of the politically correct name of "Native Americans". I felt that the name "Native Americans" could never replace the name Indians because America was formed in 1776, and the Indians were there long before this country's formation as the United States of America.

How can the Indians claim to be Americans? America wasn't even founded until 233 years ago. I grumbled.

My mind continued to wander as I drove.

I hadn't been to Omaha since my dear Samantha went to be in heaven four years ago. As I drove my truck, I passed the time thinking of wonderful memories I had made during past years with family. My oldest son Norris was a successful attorney at a prestigious law firm in Omaha. He towered over six feet in height and wore a beard with long brown hair. He carried himself well, holding his shoulders high and walking proudly. Norris had won some very important legal cases. He had an IQ of 145 and was a hard worker. But even though Norris graduated at the top of his class as summa cum laude and Valedictorian at Yale University, I still criticized him.

I can't believe how gullible and liberal Norris is. There is no excuse for that. He is such a bright and intelligent young man, I thought to myself.

I felt my son was misguided. Norris subscribed to every idea that the *mainstream* liberal media shoved down his throat.

Damn those crazy liberal, ACLU card-carrying professors at Yale- a bunch of pompous blowhards. I blamed them for Norris's fanatical liberal philosophies, because I certainly hadn't raised him to think like that.

I thought, *it's a shame those liberal professors can't be open-minded enough to teach both sides of an issue.*

I couldn't understand why they were so biased.

How can people say that conservatives are narrow-minded when there are just as many people on the left who are not open-minded to certain beliefs? I asked myself as I thought about my son's *crazy* beliefs.

Norris was married to a photogenic woman Julie who was a successful pediatrician at the local hospital. She was almost the same height as Norris at 5'11" with medium brown hair and hazel eyes. She had a smooth, silky glowing facial complexion. Julie was a beloved and well-respected physician. She received the honor of winning *Pediatrician of the Year* two years in a row and was very gifted in her field. She graduated in the top of her class also with the summa cum laude honor but from Harvard University.

It is such a shame that she turned out to be a bleeding-heart liberal, too.

She was always feeling sorry for the homeless people who begged. She gave them money, food, and whatever they needed, even before she could afford to do so. She was a magnet for all of the indigents and helpless people. I felt she was being used by them and was very *gullible* for being such an educated woman.

Norris and Julie had met at an American Medical Association convention in New York. Julie attended on medical business and Norris on legal matters. They fell in love which produced two adorable children: four-year-old Michael and nine-year-old Sadie.

As I continued driving on highway 92, I let my mind drift to all the wonderful, vivid memories I had made with my family. But then my mind shifted back to reality. I realized I hadn't been paying attention.

Louis, you idiot, I shouted. *You're already in Omaha!*

I had missed the merge onto highway 29. I cut over to the left lane and made a U-turn so that I could head south again. I turned onto highway 370. I could feel my heart racing faster and faster. I would soon see Norris, Julie, Michael, Sadie, and the rest of my family.

Stupid slow drivers are making me late. In reality I would arrive early, around noon. The family dinner didn't start until 2 p.m.

As I turned right onto highway 370 and then onto Cedar Island Road, the anticipation of seeing my family became overwhelming. I was only two miles from my son's home. I had been daydreaming and suddenly realized that I had forgotten to pick up food.

You dummy, Louis. I can't believe that you drove all this way and didn't stop at the supermarket.

I continued on that windy two-lane Cedar Island Road. As I steered the sharp curve, I thought I was seeing things. A large object was in the road.

Was it a mirage or my eyes playing tricks on me?

As I drove closer, it appeared to be a body of a young girl lying in the middle of the road. I was traveling at about 55 miles per hour. As I slammed on the brakes, an awful squealing sound of rubber burning on the pavement could be heard for miles. I swerved my truck to keep from hitting the body. My truck came to a grinding stop a few feet away. My heart nearly stopped. The young girl appeared to be lifeless lying in the road, and I had almost run over her body.

Oh my God, my God. Think fast Louis. Is she still breathing? Is

The Contrary

she still alive? Fear coursed through my body.

I bolted out of my truck and ran to the body of the young girl. Terror struck my face. I could feel cold shivers all over. I bent down to turn her body.

No, No, dear God, how could this be? I cried out in anguish as I shook my head in disbelief.

My eyes nearly popped out of my head when I recognized her face. She was still breathing. I threw my arms around her. It was unbelievable. She was alive. She wasn't hurt.

As I embraced her, I cried with tears, "You're alive, are you okay, sweetheart?"

She replied, "Yes."

"Thank God you are alive!" But I quickly began to chastise her. "What in the world are you doing lying in the middle of the road?"

I couldn't believe that the young girl lying there was my own flesh and blood, my granddaughter, Sadie.

"That is so stupid! What a dumb thing to do to lie in the middle of the road," I shouted.

Sadie was crying in reaction to my loud, harsh words and from embarrassment.

I lifted my granddaughter, kissed her on the cheek, and held her tenderly in my arms. I carried her to my truck, so she could rest in the back seat of the extended cab. I pulled the truck to the side of the road and sat there still trembling from what had happened. There was silence.

I flashed back to the memories of holding little Sadie in my arms when she was first born. She was the cutest little girl with curly blonde hair, a wide smile, and dimples. I remembered the times she would visit at the farmhouse when she was about four years old. She would giggle and say some of the funniest things. She could already read books at four years old. She made up little songs and would recite nursery rhymes. My son and daughter-in-law would always dress her in cute little dresses and overalls. She was the joy of our lives. It made me sick to think I could've killed her today with my truck. If I had driven just a little farther, a few more feet, I would have smashed her body into pieces. I would have had to live with that tragic scene haunting me for the rest of my life.

As I comforted Sadie, I noticed a long colorful strand of beads stretched around her neck. In the center of the necklace was a beautiful cross with what resembled a sculpture of Jesus. Sadie held the cross of Jesus clutched in her hand.

I looked curiously at the necklace she seemed to cherish. My eyes studied the details of the colors and design as the silence lingered. I broke the quiet.

"What's this?"

She proudly replied, "These are my rosary beads."

"Rosary beads? What do they do?"

"They protect me from danger."

"What kind of danger?"

"When I pray with these beads, nothing will ever happen to me. I am safe and protected. I simply say some *Hail Mary's* and I know that God will keep me safe from harm."

I scratched my head, confused. I remained quiet for a while.

I had asked a lot of questions about those rosary beads. I was a diehard Methodist for over 60 years and didn't understand the Catholic Church. I believed that my religion was the only correct one and that no one else was right. It was always a big mystery to me about the fathers, priests, bishops, archbishops, popes, and the Vatican. The whole thing seemed strange to me. I never had any use for the Catholic Church and its beliefs. I never placed any importance on any objects like beads or crosses. I thought they were merely symbols, not actual articles to pray with or worship. I felt that worshipping statues was idolatry. I also believed that people were *suckers* and *gullible* to believe in such things.

"Who told you that?" I asked.

"Father Stewart said so," Sadie replied.

"What did Father Stewart tell you?"

"He said that I could test God, and God would protect me."

"You mean to tell me you were testing God when you decided to lie in the middle of the road?"

"Yes, I was testing God to see if he would keep me from being hit by a car."

"Now you know that Father Stewart didn't tell you to lie in the middle of the road," I said.

"Yes, he did," Sadie replied. "He said that God would protect me from any kind of danger through faith and prayer. These beads are what I pray with for protection."

I felt like pulling my hair out. I thought I had heard it all.

"And you believe that those beads are going to save you from getting hit by a car?"

"Yes, because I have faith. God hears my prayers and answers them."

I thought about what Sadie had said. I felt frustrated because I couldn't believe that my own granddaughter was *that gullible* to believe what she had just told me.

"Come on, Sadie, get real. You know those beads aren't going to save you. If I hadn't stopped so suddenly like I did, I would have run over you and killed you!"

I pictured a gruesome and tragic scene. I imagined what it would have felt like to tell Norris and Julie such horrific news. That was a dark and painful feeling.

"I need to get you home to your mom and dad young lady. You must promise me that you will never lie in the road again like you did or do anything else to harm yourself. This is totally unacceptable. I love you way too much to let anything like this happen to you. I could never bear the thought of losing you or killing you."

Sadie remained silent holding her head down low.

"What a stupid and dumb thing to do." I kept berating her

over and over again as I shook my head in disapproval.

When I became fixated on a topic, I would become obsessed with it.

"Wait until I tell your mom and dad what you did today. I don't know what they plan on doing to help you learn your lesson. They should spank you and take away all of your privileges for a month. But knowing them and how liberal they are, they will probably let you off scot-free."

This would be a Thanksgiving Day that I would never forget. I was still shaken. I couldn't imagine my granddaughter believing such a *foolish bunch of bull* that she could just test God, and God would reach his hand out and stop a vehicle from hitting her. I shook my head in disbelief as I pulled into the driveway of Norris's home. I opened the truck door and lifted Sadie out of the back seat. I carried her up the sidewalk to the front door and rang the bell.

How am I going to tell Norris and Julie about this?

I couldn't just smooth it over and make it look like it was no big deal. Thanksgiving was off to a terrible start. My son and daughter-in-law would need to do a lot of explaining as to why they allowed their daughter to lie in the middle of the road.

They're a bunch of diehard liberals. They will probably let her off easy. They will give her a slap on the wrist. They probably won't be too concerned.

Even if that were the case, I was still glad for the chance to see Norris and Julie. Sadie and I stood there in silence, nervously waiting for the front door to open.

CHAPTER THREE

AND THE WINNER IS

I felt like I stood for the longest time with Sadie, waiting for someone to open the front door of Norris's home. Finally, the stained glass door opened as Julie greeted me. She smiled at me and hugged me affectionately, but she looked puzzled at the sight of her daughter standing at the front door with me.

"Louis, I'm glad to see you," Julie began. "Sadie, what's wrong?"

Julie stared at the sad and embarrassed look on Sadie's face.

Sadie was tongue-tied and remained silent, holding her head down.

"Sadie, go ahead and tell her what you did," I said.

"Well…I…I…I…," Sadie mumbled.

"Spit it out, Sadie."

"Grandpa almost ran over me with his car."

"He did what?" Julie gasped.

"Yes, it's true. He found me lying in the middle of the road."

"And what were you doing lying in the middle of the road, young lady?"

"I was testing God with my rosary beads. God would never

let me die—I prayed and held these beads in my hands."

Julie shook her head in disbelief. "That's crazy. I never taught you those things."

Norris and Julie took their children to the neighborhood Catholic Church. They faithfully attended Sunday school, but Julie never remembered anyone at the church teaching the use of rosary beads to test God. This was all new to her. She didn't understand what rosary beads were and how you could use them.

"Where did you learn to test God with rosary beads?"

"Father Stewart told me that the beads with prayer and faith could keep me protected from danger."

"You must have misunderstood Father Stewart. He would never tell you to lie in the middle of the road and risk dying."

Julie wrapped her arms around Sadie to comfort her.

"You are one lucky girl. You are lucky to be alive. Just so you will learn your lesson to never do such a foolish thing as this again, I am sending you to your room. Don't come out until I tell you to."

"Yes ma'am," Sadie replied as she ran upstairs.

Julie's actions in punishing Sadie took me by surprise. I had expected Julie to give Sadie a slap on the wrist. Julie was usually very lenient in discipline. But I figured that since Sadie's life was at stake, Julie came down on her harder than usual.

"Louis, can I get you something to drink?" Julie asked.

"Yes, I could use a drink right about now. I'll have a gin and tonic. I've had one heck of a day, almost running over Sadie and all."

"I'm sure it's been hard on you. I would feel the same way."

"I still can't believe I almost ran over her. That was a stupid thing to do," I said.

"Yes, I know how you feel. I know it must have scared you badly."

"It did. I love Sadie so much. You know I would never do

anything to harm or hurt her."

"Yes, I know you would never hurt her. I'm thankful that you stopped before she was injured or killed. Thank you for saving her. It's all over now. Sadie is safe thanks to you," Julie said. "Make yourself at home. Norris went to pick up some things at the store and will be back soon."

Julie brought me a gin and tonic with crackers and a port wine cheese spread.

I decided to stretch and relax on the leather couch by the fireplace in the family room. I took several long deep breaths.

No sooner than I had gotten comfortable, a statuesque young man with long dark hair, a goatee, and wire-rim glasses entered the room. He looked a bit untidy with his shirt tails out, ragged jeans, and old army boots. He was rather flamboyant with his hand and arm gestures.

"What's up, Uncle Lou, do you remember me?" The young man asked.

"How could I forget you?" I replied, "You're my nephew Adrian, the artist. Last time I saw you, you were going to that art school in St. Louis."

"You're right," Adrian replied as he swung his hands and arms dramatically in the air as if he were directing a symphony orchestra.

"Did you ever finish school?"

"Yes," Adrian said proudly.

"Well, what are you doing with your art degree?"

"It's funny you should ask. I'm still in St. Louis, trying to make a living with my art."

"That will be the day, when you make a living with art," I chuckled.

"Well, it has been a struggle. I live in this small apartment in a not-so-great neighborhood. But the rent is cheap. I've been trying to sell some of my paintings on display at one of the local downtown coffee shops. But it's tough. People don't have money to spend on the arts," Adrian confessed. "But, that's all about to change," Adrian said as he lifted his head and arms high toward the ceiling with jubilation.

"Well, tell me about it."

I never liked Adrian. I never took him seriously about anything. I always thought of Adrian as a flaky kind of dreamer, a pothead, shifty, and a total loser. In my eyes, he was a *flaming liberal*. When Adrian was a boy, he would drift from one thing to the next. He couldn't focus on anything. Adrian was always getting into trouble at school, bullying other kids and starting fights. It looked as if Adrian would never do anything with his life. Then he surprised everyone and discovered art at age 13.

"About a year ago, I got this letter in the mail," Adrian said as he held onto it for dear life. Adrian had been carrying that letter around with him ever since he had received it.

"It's a very important letter signed by the president of the National Sweepstakes," Adrian declared as he waived the document around in the air proudly.

"You mean the National Sweepstakes Company that you see advertised on television with a prize patrol?"

"Yes, that's the one."

"So what happened?"

"The letter said that I was a finalist in the ten million dollar sweepstakes drawing. It said that I had won ten million dollars," Adrian said as he stood with his arms raised high as if he were acting out a dramatic play on stage.

"It said that all I had to do was order a few magazines. So I did. I ordered some of my favorite art magazines, sent them the money, and didn't hear anything for a while. Then one day another letter came, which looked really official. It had a gold seal on the award, and said that I had won ten million dollars," Adrian proudly exclaimed as he pulled the letter out of his pocket to show me.

"The award certificate said I needed to order a few more

magazines so that I could remain the finalist. So, I did. I ordered some more magazines and sent them money."

"You've got to be kidding me, right? What have you been smoking?" I asked as I chuckled at such foolishness. I couldn't believe what I was hearing. I couldn't believe how *gullible* Adrian was.

"I kid you not. Ever since I received those official letters and award certificates about winning ten million dollars, I haven't been able to sleep much. I've contacted a realtor, and he has been helping me look for a million dollar home with a swimming pool and a Jacuzzi," Adrian confessed.

"Soon I'm going to be living the lifestyle of the rich and famous."

I laughed out loud at Adrian.

"It's time for us poor people to reclaim our wealth from those greedy, filthy rich bastards in this world," Adrian continued as he waved his arms around as if to celebrate victory.

I shook my head at such foolishness. I thought Adrian must be high on something, maybe pot, crack, or cocaine.

"Let me stop you right there," I interrupted as I stood up to protest.

"If you fall for that, you'll fall for anything," I pointed my finger at Adrian and lectured him.

"And many of those greedy, filthy rich people you talk about earned their money through plenty of hard work, blood, sweat, and tears. Those greedy, filthy rich people that you are trashing earned their money honestly."

"Most of them didn't really earn it, they stole it," Adrian said.

"No way," I scoffed at Adrian's derogatory remarks about wealthy people. I leaned my body and face closer to Adrian's.

"But I did win ten million dollars. The filthy rich people I am talking about were born with a silver spoon in their mouths,"

Adrian shouted as though it were a fact. "It's not fair that those mothers have all of the money in this world, while others like me are struggling to get by," Adrian shouted. "There should be a way to level the playing field."

"Boohoo," I mocked. "Life isn't fair, so get over it, boy."

Intense anger filled Adrian's eyes. He stared at me as if he were looking at a deeply disturbed man. Adrian had never much cared for me. He thought of me as some highfalutin, self-righteous, judgmental man. But my rude and careless remarks cut deep into the very fiber of Adrian's soul.

"Here, let me show you the official gold seal certificate to prove it," Adrian said as he handed a document over to me to read.

"You see there, it says I won ten million dollars."

I looked at the official document. There was a pause of silence.

"It says you are a finalist in a drawing for ten million dollars," I laughed at Adrian's foolishness.

"Read the fine print. Boy, if you believe this then I've got some Malibu beach property that I will sell you for a steal."

"Say what you want to say, Uncle Lou, but I know I won ten million dollars," Adrian proudly stated as he reached his hands and arms to the ceiling in a dramatic show of expression.

"You fool, you stupid fool," I shouted at Adrian judgmentally. "I've had enough. I'm not going to listen to any more of this rubbish," I said as I started to walk out of the room laughing and somewhat perturbed.

"Go ahead and laugh, Uncle Lou. I'll be laughing all the way to the bank one day soon when I collect my ten million dollars. And, Uncle Lou, when you see me on television collecting those ten million dollars, you're going to wish you hadn't made fun of me. I'll be sipping margaritas in my Jacuzzi beside my Olympic-size swimming pool."

"Like hell you will," I retorted.

The Contrary

"You're going to wish you had believed me, and you're going to wish you had some of that cold hard cash," Adrian fired back. I stomped out the room laughing but fuming mad. I left Adrian sitting by the fireplace in the family room.

What a fool, so gullible. Here is another example of an educated liberal, who is as gullible as someone who fell off the turnip truck.

"There is a sucker born every minute," I shouted back at Adrian. "I'm glad I'm not one of *those*," I haughtily proclaimed.

You could hear Adrian mumbling under his breath, "Kiss my ass."

I was so angry at Adrian. This is not the way I had planned to spend my Thanksgiving weekend with my family.

The world already has enough gullible people. We don't need any more in this family. Will I have to face more stupid, gullible people like Adrian?

I hoped that the rest of my Thanksgiving holiday would be calm and peaceful. I already had about all that I could take in one day.

CHAPTER FOUR

LIKE FATHER, LIKE SON

I was still recovering from my argument with Adrian so I hung out in the kitchen making small talk with Julie. I had deliberately moved to get away from Adrian. I didn't care if I ever saw my nephew's face again. To me, Adrian was so obnoxious and *gullible*.

"What's for dinner?" I asked.

Before Julie could reply, my son Norris walked through the door with a bag of groceries in his arms.

My face lit up with a warm smile as I saw Norris for the first time in four years. Norris affectionately returned the smile. We embraced. Tears overcame both of us.

"I can't believe you're here, Dad," Norris said. "It's been a long time."

"It has indeed been way too long. You look so distinguished with your beard. And you're letting your hair grow out, too. You look like one of those Ivy League professors."

"Well, Dad, not exactly," Norris chuckled. "But I'm having the time of my life at the law firm. They've given me some cliffhanger cases and clients. How about you, Dad? How have you been?"

"Small town life really agrees with me, but I miss seeing you all. I wish we visited each other more often."

"We only live an hour away. We do need to see each other more often," Julie interrupted. "I know we get so caught up in our own lives that we forget to call or visit. It shouldn't be that way," Norris agreed.

"Michael and Sadie are growing up so fast that I don't want to miss everything they're doing," I said.

"Well, you're always welcome anytime," Norris replied. "Dad, put your coat on and let's walk outside. I've got something to show you."

I was curious.

We buttoned up our coats and headed toward the driveway, where a shiny new red car was parked. It was the smallest car I had ever seen. I couldn't believe the size. I wondered how anyone could fit into it.

"They call this the Intelligent car," Norris said proudly.

"How do you get anyone in there?" I asked.

"It's got enough room. But the best feature of this car is that it gets over 52 miles a gallon. Dad, you don't look so excited about my new car," Norris noticed that I looked bored and distracted.

"Say something," Norris prodded.

"What happens if you get hit by an 18-wheeler?"

"It has front and side airbags and recently passed a strict government crash test with flying colors," Norris proudly replied.

"One of those big government lies," I retorted. "You know you can't trust the government." I thought about how *gullible* my son was.

"Now wait just a minute. Where do you get your facts about this being part of *big government lies*?" Norris asked as he started to grow irritated.

"You know the government, they make up stuff as they go, cook the books, and tell us only what we want to hear," I replied.

"That's ridiculous, Dad. Who told you that bunch of crap?" Norris laughed.

"Who cares if you're saving gas if you get crushed like a tin can by a monster truck," I said.

"I care about saving gas, saving our environment, and about my carbon footprint here on Earth," Norris stated.

"Your carbon what?"

"You know the carbon footprints that everyone leaves on Mother Earth. Our pollution produces greenhouse gases."

"What kind of liberal crap are you trying to say?" I asked as I started getting more agitated.

"Dad, you see, your generation and others before yours were not very responsible with protecting Mother Earth. You and others left plenty of carbon dioxide on this planet from those big gas-guzzlers that you used to drive, not to mention all of those polluting factories. This carbon dioxide creates what we call greenhouse gases, which change the climate of the Earth and cause global warming. The Earth is getting warmer and warmer until, one day; we will all burn up with the Earth being destroyed."

I was almost speechless, "Who told you all of that garbage? Back in the 1980s, a respected news magazine predicted the freezing of this planet, an ice age. Now you're saying that we're all going to burn up alive?"

"Dad, global warming and climate change are facts."

"When did they become facts?"

"Last year The Consensus Project was formed," Norris replied, "and 97% of all climate scientists in the world agreed that there was indeed global warming and climate change occurring on this planet."

"You said 97% of all climate scientists, right?" I retorted.

The Contrary

"Well, what about the 37,000 respected climate scientists in this world who say global warning and climate change are a hoax?"

"There aren't that many climate scientists who believe that, Dad," Norris protested, raising his voice.

"Oh, yes, there are. I saw a petition on the Internet signed by 37,000 climate scientists stating that global warming and climate change are a hoax perpetrated by left-wing liberals," I vehemently replied.

"You can find anything on the Internet that will validate your point of view," Norris countered.

"If there are that many who signed that letter and if there is such a letter, those are all right-wing nut jobs, Dad."

"Wait, right-wing nut jobs just because *you* disagree?" I asked heatedly.

"Yes, uneducated, uninformed people who listen to right-wing propaganda from that entire nut job talk shows scene."

"Are you calling *me* a right-wing nut job?" I protested.

"No, Dad. I just think you're misguided. I think you're slightly off track."

"How so?"

"Well, you listen to those right-wing talk shows, and you read sensational stuff on the Internet, and you start believing that your opinions are true when they aren't. A lot of things are inaccurate that you find on the Internet, Dad. It just seems kind of gullible of you to believe that stuff you read and hear."

"Wait a minute, Son, I just read that half of the climate scientists don't believe in global warming and climate change according to a new poll. And you call global warming and climate change facts."

"What poll, Dad? Did they poll only right-wingers?"

"This was a legitimate poll, done by a respected polling company."

"Again, it's right-wing propaganda. It's all part of a vast right-wing conspiracy."

"Oh, and I suppose Al Gore has *all* of the answers," I flippantly replied. "Norris, listen to me. Use the brain God gave you. When I studied biology many light years ago, my teacher emphasized that a theory wasn't a fact until it was fully proven without a shadow of a doubt. That means that everyone has to be on board to agree that a theory is a fact—right-wingers and all. So if there is any shade of doubt whatsoever, it can't be a fact, period," I shouted. "It can't be just 97% of climate scientists agreeing that there is global warming. It has to be 100% of the scientists in agreement. Science isn't about taking a popular vote to see who wins. It is about validating a theory and a hypothesis 100%."

"Look, Dad, everyone knows global warming and climate change are facts. It's all over the news."

"Yeah, right—our crooked mainstream media. They report what they decide to report. They have politicized this so-called global warming crap," I heckled my son. "Don't you know the mainstream media has their own agenda they follow with liberal bias? It's like the media has its own template. If the news of the day doesn't fit into that template, it isn't a story. It becomes a blackout," I continued as if I knew it all.

"You mean right-wing nut jobs and those crazy conspiracy people who follow Fox News and the other right-wing news networks?"

"Look, God is in control of Earth. How do we have the nerve to say we can be God, be smarter than God, and control the climate of our planet? We're not as smart and powerful as God."

"If you believe there is a God, God would want us to be responsible and take care of Mother Earth."

"But God is still in control. This global warming, climate change bunch of crap is the greatest hoax of this century," I shouted angrily as I crossed my arms in protest.

"What a right-wing bunch of crap."

"Look, Norris, this whole global warming climate change

The Contrary

debacle is a religion. Gullible liberals are blindly following this religion without questioning it. They worship Mother Earth, trees, plants, and flowers. And now our big brother, the federal government, wants to control our lives by taxing us with a carbon tax and putting every regulation on our freedom in the name of global warming and climate change," I retorted.

"Once again, this is right-wing propaganda, right-wing crap. The right-wingers don't care anything about Mother Earth. They pollute it and destroy it through careless behavior. They have no respect for our planet," Norris continued angrily.

"You see, I can't talk to you, Norris, because you never listen."

"Neither do you, Dad."

We stormed into the house angry at each other. The tension was so thick that you could have stuck it with a fork, and it still wouldn't have released all of the anger and hot air.

Julie and the others could feel the heat. Norris and I were tight-lipped and wouldn't even look at each other. Julie, sensing that it could be a long, hard Thanksgiving Day, called everyone to the dinner table.

"It's time for our big celebration. We have a lot to be thankful for on this Thanksgiving Day," Julie said. "Everyone wash up and gather around the table to bless this scrumptious food."

It would be a long Thanksgiving Day, and everyone in the Green family was just getting started. As some would say, we were just getting warmed up. But what we didn't know was that our Thanksgiving dinner was about to end abruptly by tragedy.

CHAPTER FIVE

THE THANKSGIVING DAY TRAGEDY

The Green family gathered around the long table to say grace. We stood and joined hands around the smorgasbord of food.

"Uncle Hershel, will you please say grace?" Julie asked as she bowed her head.

"Our God, sweet and merciful one, thank you for all that you have given us in our lives. We are grateful for our family, our health, our prosperity, and the time we have together. Bless this food to the nourishment of our bodies. Amen."

"Please pass the potatoes and the rolls," Aunt Hilda insisted.

Aunt Hilda appeared to be starving. She asked to be served immediately. Aunt Hilda took a whopping helping of mashed potatoes, which filled her plate. She helped herself to four rolls, which didn't leave many for the others.

"Go ahead and stuff yourself, you're a growing girl," I rudely shouted to her.

The room grew silent with embarrassment as everyone pretended that I hadn't said anything.

"Don't worry, Aunt Hilda, I have plenty more for everyone," Julie apologetically said as she broke the silence.

Julie hurried into the kitchen to get some rolls and a few more dishes to serve.

Aunt Hilda was my sister who was married to Uncle Hershel. Hilda was a large woman, well over 350 pounds. Some people would call her a woman of statue. Some would describe her as downright obese. Herschel was over six feet in height and a slender man of about 150 pounds. They were quite contrasting as a couple.

Hilda was a well-respected middle school teacher in Omaha and was loved by everyone at her school. Hilda spoke with a voice of authority and attitude. She was a generous and loving person. There were times she would tell jokes that would leave everyone rolling on the floor laughing uncontrollably.

Hershel was a pastor at the First Church of God in Omaha. He had a quiet, soft-spoken voice. He was more of the serious type but also sensitive and took comments people said to heart. He was a dedicated and loving preacher. Pastor Hershel was loved by his fellow church members. Even though Hershel and Hilda were complete opposites, they were a loving couple, happily married for forty years.

After my snide comment to Hilda, I decided not to speak to anyone else, including my son. Norris and I were in our own little world. We were still pouting over our argument.

Sadie wasn't talking either. She was still recovering from her rosary bead episode where I almost ran over her with my truck. Adrian was still sulking from his debate with me over his winning ten million dollars in the magazine sweepstakes.

No one in the family appeared to be looking at each other.

The only folks talking were Julie and Norris's four-year-old son Michael, who was playing with his food and shooting peas with his fork at his sister across the table and Sadie, who was teasing her younger brother by kicking his feet under the table. Julie was trying to keep the conversation going with small talk about the weather. She carefully avoided anything about religion, politics, or anything controversial.

Then Cousin Tyler from Atlanta, piped up, "Can you believe what our President is doing to our country? He is destroying it."

"I don't think you want to go there," Tyler's wife Amy chimed in.

"Why not? It's true," Tyler replied.

"Because I'm not in the mood to argue with your right-wing idiotology, that's why." *Idiotology* was a word Amy used to refer to those "gullible, ignorant right-wing nuts" that crossed her path.

"Well, he's right," I suddenly interrupted as I defended Tyler.

The conversations quickly ended. There was a long period of silence. It appeared no one wanted to participate in that conversation. No one wanted to go down that road, where they couldn't win in an argument.

Everyone had been served and seemed to be enjoying the turkey, mashed potatoes, rolls, and green beans. But you could tell that not everyone was having a good time.

"Could you please pass me some seconds?" Hilda asked before she continued. "I've discovered a revolutionary new diet pill."

"What's it called? Where did you hear about it?" Julie asked.

"I saw it on television." Hilda said as she chomped down on more rolls and turkey.

Hilda was eating faster than anyone else. She had already helped herself to one large plate and was going for seconds.

"Dr. U on his television show endorses it. It's called the amazing yucca pill," Hilda mumbled with food in her mouth.

"You mean the famous Dr. U?" Julie asked. "I've never heard of the yucca pill."

"Yes, Dr. U says it really works. It's made from a leaf of a plant only found in South America near the Amazon River," Hilda replied.

The Contrary

"But, Hilda, you've tried over a dozen different diets, and so far none of them have worked," Hershel chimed in.

"Shut up, Hershel. You don't know what you're talking about. This pill is so magical that you can eat all you want every day and all the time, and you still lose weight," Hilda said as she marveled at the advertised results. "You don't need to exercise, and you can lose weight while you sleep."

There was silence as everyone tried to digest Hilda's remarks, but the silence was broken with a sudden roar of laughter, which made Hilda angry. Some were trying not to laugh at Hilda, but her statements about losing weight without exercise and dieting were so absurd. We couldn't help but laugh.

"How can you believe all of that crap?" I asked.

"I believe the same way that you believe all of your right-wing propaganda," Hilda shot back. "Don't start on me, Louis. Why, I've already lost 20 pounds."

"Yeah, and you'll gain it all back today," Hershel shouted jokingly.

Hilda's face turned beet red. She was getting angrier and angrier from all of the ridicule.

"Why doesn't anyone believe me when I say that this miracle diet pill works? I see you with smirks on your faces laughing at me. Wipe those smirks off your faces right now."

Hilda kept eating faster and faster as she was talking. She was trying to get as much food into her mouth as she possibly could. She made all kinds of noises while she ate. She was smacking, burping, slurping, and chomping.

It really got on my nerves.

Here we go again — another gullible family member. Our family is no different than the 95 percent of the gullible people in this world.

Hilda interrupted everyone as she attempted to speak with a helping of food in her mouth. You could barely hear what she was saying.

"Wait till you see me next year, I'm going to be…" Hilda mumbled as she gasped for breath.

She began choking violently. Hilda had a piece of food stuck in her windpipe and kept coughing, trying to clear her throat. Hilda had turned blue in the face and looked helpless as she was fighting for her life.

Hershel reached from the back to try to perform the Heimlich maneuver on her. But his arms had trouble reaching around her. Nevertheless, he kept trying desperately to save his wife.

Norris opened Hilda's mouth and tried his best to clear her throat with his fingers but she was still choking. Everyone was in a state of panic.

I called 911 demanding that the paramedics hurry to the house. Everyone stood over her feeling helpless. Some were trying to help, while some were in the way. Others just stared.

"Someone help her," Sadie shouted again as she started crying. "We can't let her die."

Julie wasn't as experienced in the area of paramedics because she was a pediatrician. But Julie acted fast.

"Someone find some cardboard," Julie shouted.

Julie carefully and steadily took a small kitchen knife and cut a hole in Aunt Hilda's lower esophagus near her windpipe.

"Get me some washcloths. Heat them up in the microwave."

"Don't just sit there, help her," Sadie shouted.

While the washcloths were boiling in the microwave, Julie was applying pressure to the newly cut wound in Hilda's windpipe to cauterize it.

I opened the microwave and handed her the piping hot cloths. Julie applied them to the fresh wound. She cut a piece of cardboard and made what resembled a medium-sized tube. She placed it through the newly cut area of Hilda's windpipe. It appeared that Hilda wasn't breathing or responding. Julie gave her oxygen through the makeshift cardboard tube. Time seemed

The Contrary

to stand still. The paramedics rushed through the door to the dining room where Hilda was lying. They worked on clearing her throat and gave her an oxygen mask. They lifted her onto a stretcher to place her into the ambulance. The others stood there helplessly watching in shock, not saying a word.

The family huddled together and held each other sobbing.

"I'll see you all at the hospital," Hershel said while solemnly hanging his head down.

"I hope she will be alright, Uncle Hershel," Julie said.

"She'll live," I said.

"What hospital are they taking her to?" Norris asked.

"She's going to Methodist Hospital." Hershel stepped into the back of the ambulance where Hilda was lying. They whisked her away at lightning speeds. The other family members rushed to put their coats on and jumped in their cars to hurry to the hospital.

Many of the family members felt bad for what they had said about Hilda's miracle diet pill. They felt awful about how they had laughed and ridiculed her. In fact, everyone was feeling guilty about the incident except for me. I was the only one who didn't feel sorry for her. I thought that she had brought it on herself because she had made herself fat. Also, she had been talking with a full helping of food in her mouth. She had been eating twice as fast as everyone else and had eaten everything in sight. It was the moment of truth. We would soon find out if Aunt Hilda would live or die. This would be a long Thanksgiving as we prepared for a long wait at the hospital.

CHAPTER SIX

CAMPING OUT IN THE ER

Norris and Julie sped off in their car, headed west toward Methodist Hospital. I was right behind them. I followed them all the way to the Emergency Room. All of the other family members were *en route*, too. Hershel had arrived with the ambulance before anyone else. Fear struck his body as the paramedics lifted her stretcher out of the ambulance and rushed her into the ER. Hershel worried about whether his wife would make it or not in that ER.

Norris and Julie, along with their two children, parked their car and hurried into the hospital arrival area. When they arrived at the front desk, they encountered a prim and proper nurse. She resembled an army sergeant with horn-rimmed glasses and seemed quite uncaring. Her words were curt. She was too busy to help anyone as her ear was glued to the phone.

"Um, um," Norris cleared his throat as he tried to get her attention. "We are looking for Hilda Campbell."

The nurse was unresponsive. She seemed to be in her own world carrying on her own phone conversation.

"We are looking for Hilda Campbell," Norris shouted.

"I heard you the first time," the nurse dryly replied, clearly perturbed. She hung up the phone and typed on her computer keyboard.

"She's in ER room four."

Norris rushed passed her toward the ER ward.

"Sir, sir, you can't go back there," the nurse shouted.

"Why can't I?" Norris asked.

"You can't because no one is allowed there at this time."

Norris ignored her and opened the ER door.

"Security, security."

Immediately, two security guards grabbed Norris by the arms.

"Is this necessary?" Norris threatened, "I'm an attorney, and I'm going to sue your ass if you don't let me go."

"Sir, calm down," the security guards said as they escorted him to the waiting room and sat him in a chair.

"Don't tell me to calm down. My Aunt Hilda is fighting for her life back there, and you can't even let me see her."

About that time, I had arrived with other family members.

Norris was fed up with the nurse and the security guards. But he didn't want to make a scene in front of family. He didn't want to receive a judgmental tongue-lashing from me with my judgmental ways.

Norris remained seated in the waiting room along with everyone else. Hershel and Adrian were the only ones missing. They knew Hershel was with Hilda, but no one knew exactly where Adrian was.

"Maybe he's smoking a joint and getting high," I said.

"What an awful thing to say about your nephew," Julie piped up.

I gave her a disapproving eye in return.

It was only 3:30 p.m. but it felt like midnight because of all we had been through.

Time passed. The clock on the wall read 6:30 p.m.

There was no word from anyone about Hilda's condition.

"I'm worried about Adrian. Something's not right. He should have been here by now. Maybe we should call him," Julie said.

"I'm sure he is fine. He probably had something important to do," Norris replied.

"But he told us that he would come see Hilda at the hospital. That was four hours ago. I know how much he loves Hilda," Julie continued with a worried voice.

"Well, if it easies your mind, Julie, I will call Adrian right now."

Norris called Adrian several times but got no answer, not even his voice mail message. Norris sent a text to Adrian, but there was no reply.

"Whatever he's doing, he's busy right now because he's not answering his calls or text messages," Norris tried to reassure Julie.

"Norris, something has happened to Adrian. I just know. He always answers his text messages," Julie said anxiously.

"Sweetheart, please don't worry. Adrian will be fine. I'm sure something came up, and he had to attend to it," Norris tried to ease her worries.

After their conversation about Adrian's whereabouts, Norris and Julie had nothing more to say to each other. There was complete silence between them.

Time passed as the clock read 9:30 p.m. There was still no word about Hilda.

Everyone waiting seemed to be bored. Some family members were whistling to kill time. Some were humming tunes, tapping their feet, or twiddling their thumbs. A few were pacing the floor, and some were stretched out half asleep. The children were picking on each other and calling each other names. They were running around the ER waiting room and had to be called down a number of times by security. They were

The Contrary

"kids" and they had no patience to wait for any length of time. They wanted to be home playing in their own rooms.

Cousin Janie from Chicago broke the long silence.

She handed Norris, Julie and me some colorful printed magazines.

"What's this?" Norris asked.

"This is our magazine *The Watchtower*," Janie proudly replied.

"Oh, brother, she's a Witness. That's just what we need," I quirked sarcastically, before rudely shouting at her, "You bunch of *gullible* fools."

"Now be nice," Julie calmly said to me.

"How can I be nice to someone who is going around spreading fiction and lies?" I shouted back at Julie.

Cousin Janie cringed. Her face turned red and her muscles tightened over the rude remarks.

Julie and I tried to hand the magazines back to her.

"Just wait a minute. Keep an open mind," Janie said as she raised her voice at Julie and me.

"This magazine is filled with powerful suggestions on how to live our lives fully through Jehovah's plan."

"Don't get me started on that cult crap," I said. "Once you become a Witness you can never leave their cult. And if you are lucky to leave, you are dead to them."

"You actually believe all that garbage?" Norris asked.

"Of course I do. And don't call it garbage," Janie replied. "Every bit is true. You see the *King James Bible* and all of the other bibles that you read today are incorrectly translated. We use the Greek translated *Bible*, which is far more accurate than the others."

"That's because those bibles are written to support your made-up bunch of bull. You have to use your own made-up *Bible*.

What's wrong with the *King James Bible?*" I stood and pointed my finger in Janie's face.

"Louis, you don't have to be so rude about it. She is a member of our family," Julie interrupted.

Janie appeared stunned by my rudeness and curtness. It was as if she had stirred up a hornet's nest, and suddenly they were swarming all over her. She listened to me for a few minutes, hoping I would calm down and come to my senses.

"And you believe that Jesus came back to this planet in the 1940s and that he's walking the streets of New York City," I laughed in Janie's face.

Everyone stopped talking and there was silence. It was obvious that Janie was feeling the heat from me, and she was becoming humiliated by my anger, sarcasm, and hostility toward her. Janie took a deep breath, tried to regain her composure, and then spoke again.

"Well, I don't know about Jesus walking the streets of New York City. But I do know that Jesus is supposed to return to Earth invisibly as he left the Earth. So I believe that Jesus has already returned to Earth," Janie confidently said.

"So why haven't I seen him?" I mocked her flippantly.

"Yeah, like isn't the whole world supposed to see Him arrive on a mighty cloud?" Norris asked.

"The Greek translation of the *Bible* says that he left this Earth invisible and will return invisible," Janie quipped. "He came to this Earth in 1948, the same year that Israel became a nation."

"There you go again, using your own crazy Greek *Bible*," I shouted heatedly. "The date of Jesus' return has been changed several times: 1874, 1914 and 1948. How many more times are you going to change the date, so that it can conveniently fit in with what you believe?" I asked.

The Contrary

"This time we're right on..." Before Janie could complete her sentence, she was interrupted by Katy Beth, one of the nieces in the family.

"We have our own *Bible*, too, but it's not made up," Katy Beth said proudly as she flipped her head from side to side.

"Let me guess, Mormon?" I flippantly asked.

"Well, that's what some people refer to us as. But we are really called Jesus Christ of Latter Day Saints.

"Oh, yes, I know all about it. I used to be friends with a whacko Mormon," I said sarcastically. "You use the *Book of Mormon* instead of the *Bible*."

"We use both," Katy Beth corrected me. "The *Book of Mormon* was given to our prophet Joseph Smith on tablets."

"Oh, yeah, you mean the Joseph Smith who was supposedly visited by an angel?" I laughed.

"Yes, that Joseph Smith, and he was visited by an angel a long time ago," Katy Beth defended.

"The *Book of Mormon* was plagiarized from an old novel about North America and the Indians," Janie quipped testily.

"Who told you that?" Katy Beth asked, offended by Janie's remark.

"I read it on some website," Janie replied.

"Surely you don't believe everything you read on websites," Katy Beth shot back.

"You people believe that after Jesus resurrected, he returned to Earth and walked the land of North America. You believe that the Garden of Eden is in Missouri right?" I grilled her.

"Yes, you are correct in that," Katy Beth acknowledged.

"It doesn't say a word about Jesus visiting North America in the *King James Bible*. It says that Jesus went to sit at the right hand of the Father who is in heaven after he resurrected," I said flippantly as if I knew it all.

"Our *Book of Mormon* recounts Jesus visiting North America after his resurrection," Katy Beth replied, trying to stay calm.

"The Mormons are very family oriented," Katy said proudly.

"And you are prolific, kind of like Catholics," I blurted out loud.

Katy Beth smiled and laughed under her breathed about my comment on being prolific.

"We're not exclusive like you Witnesses are of saying only 144,000 are going to be spared in the end times," Katy Beth emphatically stated.

"That 144,000 is only an estimate," Janie responded.

"Well, even if there were one million Witnesses spared in the end times, what happens to the billions of the world population?" Katy Beth shot back.

There was silence. Janie appeared to be tongue-tied in responding to Katy Beth's last question of what would happen to most of the world population in the end times.

"And you don't believe that there's a heaven or hell," Katy Beth said. "You basically don't believe that a human being has a soul period."

"Yes, that's right. We believe that once you die you rot in the ground—dust to dust," Janie defended herself.

"How crazy is that. We don't have souls," I mocked as I moved my head from side to side.

"We Mormons believe that we go to heaven after we die," Katy Beth interjected.

"You go to some crazy planet called Kolob," I shouted

"It's not a planet but a star where we will live forever," Katy Beth answered.

"And you believe that you will become gods equal to God," I replied. "How blasphemous is that."

"Thou shall have no other Gods but me. That's what one of the commandments in the Bible says," I said confidently. "And what is your belief on the act of salvation? Do you believe that someone can be saved?" I asked.

"We believe that hard work here on Earth saves us," Katy

Beth replied.

"Unbelievable. So you don't believe in salvation even though Jesus was nailed to the cross for our sins?" I asked.

"We believe Jesus died for our sins, but we believe our hard work on Earth saves us," Katy Beth replied.

"So then why did Jesus go to all the trouble to be humiliated in his crucifixion for our sins if we have to work like slaves to be saved?" I asked flippantly.

"The *Book of Mormon* is very clear about us working hard to perfect ourselves to be like God so that we will be saved in the end," Katy Beth replied confidently. Suddenly there was a silence just like the calm before a violent storm.

"I can't go anywhere without running into such foolish, *gullible* people." I shouted in a fit of rage as I stood on the waiting room chair pointing my finger at Katy Beth and Janie.

"And to think my whole family is full of them," I continued shouting.

A security guard heard me loudly ranting and raving. He hurried into the ER waiting room and reprimanded me.

"If you do it again, I am going to call the police and have you arrested," he warned me.

I stepped down from the chair, embarrassed by the security guard. I took a deep breath and tried to calm myself down. I took a seat in the chair I had been standing on.

At that very moment a stranger who was sitting in the ER waiting room moved closer to Norris, Julie and me.

"I couldn't help but overhear your conversation about all of those religious points of view," he commented. "I don't have any use for any of those religions. My religion is so much more advanced than any of yours."

"So what have you got that they don't?" I flippantly replied as I tried to remain calm.

"Our spirit is immortal. We have lived many lives before in different bodies," the stranger claimed.

"Let me guess—Hinduism?" I asked sarcastically.

"No. We are way more sophisticated than that. We can actually learn how to control our brains so that we control anything in our lives," the stranger said.

Everyone remained silent and listened.

"It's called Dianetics. It is the use of science to help us reach our full potential in life."

"Yes, and it was all founded by a science fiction writer named L. Ron Hubbard," I laughed. "This means he made the whole religion up."

"No, really, this is the truest form of religion. And it really works. It is called the Church of Scientology," the stranger said confidently.

"You have a secret temple where all your cult members do weird and strange things," I quipped.

"It may seem to you like a cult, but it isn't. It's the only true form of religion in this world," the stranger retorted.

I couldn't take it anymore with all these *gullible* people and their *whacky* religions.

I stood up in front of the entire crowd of my family and others in the ER waiting room and folded my arms in protest.

"Why can't religions just be plain and simple like the Methodists do it? I don't need all that extra crap you are teaching. You are a bunch of *gullible* people to believe all these views that I've heard in the last hour. Gullible, gullible, gullible. Read my lips," I screamed. "That's it. I am done with you crazy people."

I walked away from the crowd and found a corner of my own to sit in.

Those religious nut jobs had tested every ounce of patience I had left inside me. I hadn't come to the hospital to argue religion. I had come to learn about Hilda's condition.

Everyone was dumbfounded. They were speechless over my childish antics and gross display of self-righteousness and hypocrisy.

The security guard rushed into the ER waiting room again and grabbed me by my arms.

"I warned you about disturbing the peace in this hospital and you ignored me," the security guard said as he handcuffed me. Norris and Julie rushed to my defense.

"Sir, please let him go. I promise you that he will not be rowdy anymore. We will see to it," Julie pleaded with the security guard to release me.

"Okay, I suppose, ma'am, if you both promise not to let this crazy guy out of your sight, and you promise to keep him quiet," the security guard replied.

Julie and Norris thanked the security officer for showing mercy on me. They escorted me to a chair in the waiting room and sat me in between the two of them.

I thought I had been arguing religion for an hour. In reality it had been over four hours. The clock on the wall now read almost 2 a.m. and everyone was half asleep. It had become very quiet and still after all the heated exchanges of religious talk. I was drained from my rowdy antics and verbal gymnastics. I dosed off to sleep for a while.

Suddenly, a handsome, dark-haired man dressed in medical scrubs came out of the ER ward. Hershel followed him, and he woke the family.

"Is this the family of Hilda Campbell?" The doctor asked.

"Yes," some said as they shook their heads.

When I saw what was going on my eyes opened wide, I stood from my chair and hurried over to join my family, who were talking with the doctor.

"I am Doctor Tobias," the man introduced himself. "Hilda Campbell is in critical condition. She has been admitted to the CCU Unit."

"What happened to her?" Norris asked.

"Apparently some food got lodged in her windpipe and she

nearly choked to death," Dr. Tobias said. "One of you brave souls cut a hole in her esophagus to give her oxygen to breathe."

"That would be me. I don't know if I would call the act brave. I was trying to save her life," Julie piped up.

"You did the right thing," Dr. Tobias replied.

"What is Hilda's condition?" Norris asked.

"Not good. The stress on her body without oxygen for a length of time caused her to experience a severe stroke. She is unconscious, and we have her on life support," the doctor said apologetically. "I am sorry to have to break this unfortunate news to you."

"Is she going to make it?" Julie asked.

"She has a 15 percent chance of recovering. Her body is weak and her organs are not working properly," he replied.

Hershel appeared to be a wreck. He had fallen apart, and his face was filled with deep anguish.

"We will continue to monitor her and do everything possible in our hands to help her," Dr. Tobias said with compassion.

After that news, everyone gathered around Hershel to console and encourage him. Members of the family wrapped their arms around Hershel. They prayed for him. It was a sight to see; family members wrapped around Hershel in a circle praying for him in the ER waiting room. Many of the family members decided it was time to leave and head back home. They were trying to find a graceful way to exit without hurting Hershel. They bid their farewells, hugging and kissing each other, thanking Norris and Julie for inviting them to the Thanksgiving dinner.

The only people left at the ER were Norris, Julie, Michael, Sadie, Uncle Hershel, Cousin Janie, Niece Katy Beth and me. We decided to stay a little longer to support Hershel. But when the clocked turned 5 a.m., we all decided to leave the hospital and head home.

Julie worried about Adrian's whereabouts. It had been

The Contrary

almost 14 hours since they had last talked. She was sure that Adrian would come to the hospital to join the family. She knew how much Adrian loved and cared for Hilda. Julie knew in her heart that something bad had happened to Adrian. She and Norris had tried to reach him many times by calling him and texting him. It was not like Adrian to ignore their calls and text messages.

Adrian's whereabouts would continue to worry her until she knew he was safe.

Norris, Julie, Michael Sadie and I all headed back to Norris's house. We reassured Hershel that Hilda would recover. We hugged and kissed Hershel, Janie, and Katy Beth. I had planned on spending Thanksgiving weekend with my son and daughter-in-law. I was in no shape to drive back to my farmhouse in Griswold.

Finally, we received news on Hilda, and we could leave the hospital, which felt like a prison to us. We were tired and hungry. We were ready for some sleep. Little did we know that a disaster was brewing on the horizon, waiting when we got home.

CHAPTER SEVEN

TOTAL DESTRUCTION

As Norris, Julie, the children and I headed home; Hilda remained continuously on our minds. We worried that she wouldn't make it. We thought about what would happen to Hershel if she were to pass. A million thoughts raced through our minds. But what we were about to walk into wouldn't have crossed our minds in a thousand years. We were too busy being preoccupied with Hilda's fragile condition.

I was the first to arrive at Norris and Julie's home. I parked my truck in the driveway and walked the front sidewalk to their house. I thought it was mighty strange that the beautiful stained glass front door was standing wide open. It was twilight and the sun would soon rise. There wasn't a light on in the house. I remembered that when we had left hurriedly to the hospital, we had left every light on. I became suspicious. I ran to my truck to get my pistol. As I was about to enter the pitch-black house, Norris, Julie, and the children parked their car behind my truck in the driveway. Julie noticed that I was holding a gun in my hands.

"Louis, what the hell are you doing with that gun?" Julie

The Contrary

asked tensely. "Guns make me nervous. They kill people."

"Guns don't kill people. People kill people," I retorted.

"Put away that gun, Dad."

"Quiet, there is someone inside the house," I whispered as I entered the doorway.

I held my pistol firmly in my hands with my finger over the trigger. Step by step, I walked carefully through the pitch-black house. Norris and Julie followed me. The children were asleep in the car in the driveway. We tiptoed quietly through the foyer searching for a light switch.

I thought I heard a noise. *Someone was still in the house.* I motioned to Norris and Julie to remain quiet and to look around their shoulders for anything that moved. I proceeded cautiously with my finger on the trigger of my gun. We fumbled around until finally I found the switch and turned on the living room lights. My eyes opened wide with shock. I became nauseous and sick to the pit of my stomach by what caught my eyes.

Julie froze in her tracks and screamed at the top of her lungs. Norris was in shock, totally flabbergasted. We stopped and stared.

"Shh...keep quiet," I whispered.

Animals, I angrily said to myself.

What kind of animals would do such a thing? I continued thinking as I grew more and more agitated.

I helplessly shook my head.

"They could still be here," I whispered as I quietly searched the area, aiming my pistol at the wall as I crept around the room.

"I seriously doubt it," Norris whispered. "Who would stick around after doing this much damage? They have long gone."

Julie was in a state of shock. Her face had terror written all over it. The newly painted yellow walls in the living room were spray-painted with obscenities. There were phrases like "eat the rich" and "death to the greedy" smeared in brown human excrement. Every word that started with an "f" or an "s" was spray-painted into a collage of graffiti. Everything that was made of glass was shattered into a million pieces scattered everywhere. There were remains of lamps, vases, and leather sofas all carved up into bits and pieces. Every furniture item was turned upside down and cut up.

Norris and I made our way to the kitchen and turned on the lights. Every single china dish and plate was smashed and crushed into fragments scattered everywhere on the wooden floor. The valuable silverware was missing. The silver tea trays and cups were gone. Their butcher knives and sharp kitchen knives were stuck into the light blue painted walls with blood smeared around the targeted areas.

Norris and I thought it might be real human blood smeared on the kitchen walls. What we discovered was inhumane and absolutely gross.

Julie screamed hysterically as she opened the pantry door. Norris threw up as he looked like he had seen a ghost. Lying on one of the pantry shelves was the severed head of the children's favorite black Persian cat. The rest of the cat's body was cut up into pieces scattered around the pantry. There were guts and organs hanging off the pantry shelves. The pantry reeked with the smell of death. There were flies swarming around the decapitated head. The eyes of the dead cat were protruding with the eyes of terror. Apparently the cat had been caught by surprise by its psychopathic murderer.

"This is totally sick," Norris cried.

"Whoever did this should get the electric chair," I shouted.

It appeared that the kitchen knives were used to cut the cat into pieces. The blood from the cat was smeared all over the walls. There were flies stuck to the wall, and flies swarming around the wall where the blood was smeared.

Buckets of orange paint were thrown all over the other walls and on the maple floors.

The Contrary

As Julie, Norris and I made our way around the different areas of the house, it was the same scene in every room. Everything was smashed into millions of pieces, and everything was totally mutilated beyond recognition. There were spray-painted obscenities and graffiti on every single wall of the house.

Norris and Julie were thankful their children were asleep in the car and didn't have to see such destruction.

"Whoever did this did it all in less than 12 hours," Norris said angrily.

"They must have known that we weren't at home," Julie said as she was still in a state of shock.

"It's despicable," I said heatedly.

"This wouldn't have happened if you two had locked your doors and had not been such trusting souls!" I shouted. "You are such naïve and *gullible* folks."

Suddenly there was silence as anger welled up inside Norris and Julie.

"How could you say such insensitive, hurtful words?" Norris asked me.

"Well, it's true. You haven't locked your doors in years. You are so trusting and naïve, believing that you live in such a safe neighborhood that no one would ever do such a thing as what happened today," I self-righteously proclaimed.

Again, silence.

"Such gullible fools."

Julie was the first one to speak, "Okay, Louis, I've had it with you and your judgmental attitude."

I remained quiet as Julie tore into me with her angry words and bitter emotions.

"Careful, Julie, don't say anything you'll regret later," Norris cautioned.

"Shut up, Norris. You and I both know this needs to be addressed. We have been walking on eggshells for years with your dad. We have worried about not hurting his feelings and pandering to his nonsensical whims," Julie continued as she raised her voice. "I'm fed up with him and his disrespectful attitude. He is nothing but a lonely, angry, and bitter old man."

Julie continued ranting as if I was not even in the room.

"He is angry at the world. He has no friends because he judges everyone and thinks he is perfect. He thinks he is better than everyone else and doesn't have respect for anyone else's opinion."

"Are you finished?" Norris asked in a calm voice.

"No, I'm not," Julie replied. "I can't stand to be around your dad."

"You really mean that?" I asked softly.

"Well, for right now, I do."

Everyone became quiet. It was an awkward situation for Norris, Julie, and me.

How can you take something hurtful back that you said about someone you are supposed to love? Norris thought.

Then Norris and I headed upstairs to the bedrooms. Julie followed.

Everyone was silent. As we turned the lights on and entered the master bedroom, we stopped and stared in shock. Our eyes were glued to the bed.

Someone had torched Norris and Julie's new bed and mattress. It's a wonder the house hadn't caught on fire when the mattress had burned but it appeared to have been extinguished with water, which was spilled all over the wooden floor.

Norris and I shook our heads in disbelief.

As we entered the master bath, we noticed the bathtub Jacuzzi was still running. The perpetrators had deliberately left the water on in the bathtub. Water was running all over the floor and leaking through the ceiling below into the den. We hadn't noticed the leak downstairs because Julie, Norris and I had focused our attention on the living room and the kitchen.

The Contrary

Someone had rigged the toilet mechanism in the master bathroom so that it would overflow. The toilet was left running and had flooded the master bathroom and bedroom. There was about two inches of water standing in the master bath. It was a disaster.

Julie broke down, buried her face in her hands, and sobbed hysterically. Norris wrapped his arms around her and reassured her that everything would be okay. Julie and Norris shared some tender, private moments together as I watched them console each other.

After a while we continued searching around the house assessing the damage.

"Our safe is missing," Norris realized. "We had thousands of dollars, diamonds, gold, and bonds stored in there."

I didn't have any sympathy for them in their destruction and loss. I was angry but felt like Norris and Julie could have been more responsible in locking their doors. I kept thinking over and over how naïve and gullible my son and daughter-in-law were, especially for being such educated people.

"That's it. I'm going to find out who did this if I have to turn over every rock in this town," Norris shouted angrily. His blood boiled. "Why, God, why?"

"You can't blame God for this," I said. "It was totally your fault."

"Don't start," Julie warned as she screamed at me.

Norris reached into his pocket and pulled out his smart phone.

He dialed 911.

"This is 911, what is your emergency?"

"We've been robbed and ransacked," Norris's voice sounded panic-stricken, speaking very quickly.

"Slow down and take a deep breath," the operator commanded. "What is your location?"

"2126 Cedar Point Road," Norris replied as he tried to keep

himself together.

"I have a unit on the way," the operator answered. "Is anyone injured?"

"Our cat has been murdered," Norris shouted. "And our house looks like one giant cesspool."

"I am sorry to hear that. The officers are en route to that address. Stay calm. Everything will be okay."

Norris hung up the phone and shook his head in sadness.

While waiting for the police to arrive Norris, Julie and I made our way to Sadie's bedroom. When we turned on the lights, we were stunned. Sadie's new bedroom set had been torched, and all of Sadie's stuffed animals and dolls were cut into pieces.

"Sadie will be crushed. What do we tell her?" Julie asked sadly.

"We don't tell her anything," Norris replied calmly.

"After we file the police report, we are going to head straight down to Holiday Inn and get ourselves a room. We can't let the kids see this, and we can't live in this disaster."

When Julie, Norris and I made our way to Michael's bedroom and turned on the lights, it was more of the same. A torched bed, mutilated stuffed animals, and spray-painted obscenities all over the walls.

Suddenly, Julie, Norris, and I heard sirens and saw blue flashing lights through the upstairs window.

The police rushed in through the open front door.

"Are you Norris and Julie Green?" The officers asked.

"Yes," they both replied.

The officers moved from room to room to assess the destruction. They asked questions and were taking notes as to what items were missing.

"This is really bad," Detective Riley said with astonishment. "I've never seen anything like this in the 24 years that I've been on the Omaha police force. Things like this just don't happen around here. Have you got any enemies?"

"No, not really. I can't think of any that I would call enemies," Norris replied.

"How about you, Dad, any enemies?" Norris asked me.

I remained silent. I had been tongue-lashed by Julie, and I was still in a state of shock.

"I would suggest that you call your insurance company immediately," Detective Riley said.

The officers walked around every inch of the interior of the house and shook their heads in disbelief.

"Somebody's going to pay for all this," Detective Riley said with disgust.

"Do you think they were kids or was it a professional job?" Norris asked.

"It looks like some gang or cult members who could have done this. Your cat was murdered in a sick and violent way. There are obscenities smeared all over your walls. This looks like the mark of gang members. It's unbelievable. The worst I've ever seen," Detective Riley said. "Here's my number and email address at headquarters. Could you please make a complete list of all of the damage and the missing articles? Please send them to me as soon as possible. We will find out who did this monstrosity. They won't get away with it."

"Thank you, Detective," Norris and Julie said.

Norris and Julie were so disgusted. They went out to their car but couldn't take any clothes or suitcases with them because everything had been demolished.

I ran to start my truck.

We drove to the nearby Holiday Inn to get some rest and peace of mind from the total catastrophe of the day.

Our whole lives had been destroyed by some crazy maniac who was a psychopathic murderer. And now we had to put the pieces back together again, or so we hoped. It was only 9 a.m. Friday morning. Thanksgiving was a total wreck and our weekend had just started. We hoped our luck would soon turn around and there would be a happy ending. But our Thanksgiving was getting ready to become nothing but one disaster after another. We just didn't know it yet.

CHAPTER EIGHT

HOME AWAY FROM HOME

After the devastating Friday morning, Norris and Julie pulled into the parking lot of the nearby Holiday Inn. Julie was emotionally drained, and the children were still asleep in the car.

"Michael and Sadie wake up," Norris said as he gently nudged them on their shoulders.

They were yawning, stretching and looked confused.

"Where are we?" Sadie asked. "What are we doing in front of a hotel?"

"It's a long story," Norris replied.

"I want to go home," Michael cried.

"I want to sleep in my own bed," Sadie demanded.

"We need a little break from our house," Norris replied.

"Think of this as our vacation during Thanksgiving weekend," Norris tried to convince them. "We'll have nice beds and free breakfast while we are here. It will be home away from home."

"But what's wrong with our house?" Sadie asked.

At that moment, Norris and Julie both knew that Michael

and Sadie weren't buying their story. The children knew their mom and dad were acting strange and avoided talking to them about the house. They had to let their children in on the condition of the house someway, somehow.

"Let's go get checked into our room, and we will explain to you why we are here over breakfast," Norris said.

As everyone got out of the car and walked toward the hotel, I pulled into the parking lot in my truck.

"Is this where we are staying?" I asked.

"Yes. We are about to check in," Norris replied.

We walked into the hotel and gave our identification and credit cards to the front desk clerk. We had arranged with the hotel to stay through the Thanksgiving weekend until the following Thursday morning. Norris and Julie would have their own room with the children. Even though they weren't wild about the idea, I would have my own room adjoining theirs.

We took the elevator to the fifth floor and found our rooms: 501 and 503.

Julie, Norris, and I were so relieved to be staying in a quiet and well-kept place. This Holiday Inn was known for being one of the best hotels in Omaha. It was clean and had all of the luxuries away from home. We realized that this was just a temporary home and a quick fix to our gigantic problem back at home. Still we needed some peace of mind and some sleep. Julie and Norris were trying to figure out what to tell Michael and Sadie why they were here instead of at their own home. The cold hard truth just wouldn't be acceptable because it might scare and upset them.

"Let's get some breakfast," Julie said as she beckoned the children to head her way toward the elevator.

"I'm starving," Sadie said.

"So am I," Michael agreed.

I huddled with them into the elevator and took it to the first floor where the food was being served.

The Contrary

"Wow, a hot breakfast," I commented.

"I haven't seen this much food since yesterday," Norris joked.

As we filled our plates with eggs, bacon, waffles, fruit, and hash brown potatoes, we found a large comfortable table. I sat beside them.

We ate as quickly as we could since we hadn't eaten in a long time.

"Slow down, Michael and Sadie," Julie said.

"There's something your dad and I want to tell you regarding our house."

"Yesterday when we had to leave our house suddenly to check on Aunt Hilda, someone carelessly left the water running in the bathtub," Norris said. "Because they forgot to turn the water off, the water ran over and flooded our bathroom and our bedroom."

"I didn't do it," Sadie said defensively.

"It wasn't me," Michael said.

"Your mom and I aren't accusing you of leaving the water on," Norris said.

"We don't know who did it," Julie said. "It could've been one of our guests. What matters is that it was done and it has ruined our house."

"Also, when someone last used the toilet upstairs, the toilet got stuck and water ran all over the floor for hours," Norris said.

"There must be at least two inches of water standing in our bathroom and bedroom," Julie complained.

"Yeah and it leaked through the ceiling and ruined our downstairs floors and ceiling," Norris said.

There was a long moment of silence. Julie, Norris, Michael, and Sadie stared at each other looking helpless.

"What a crock," I blurted out as I broke the long silence.

"Half of the truth is still a lie."

Julie and Norris were startled that I would say such a thing.

"Grandpa, why don't you stay out of this?" Norris said angrily.

"Absolutely not."

"The grandkids deserve to know the truth."

"You don't know what you're talking about," Norris replied.

"I most certainly do."

Julie and Norris were stunned and felt betrayed by what I was about to say. I would devastate the children with my news and I would make Julie and Norris look bad in front of their children.

How could they ever trust their parents again? They would always believe that their parents were liars: once liars, always liars, Julie thought to herself.

"Michael and Sadie, please don't listen to Grandpa. He doesn't know what he's talking about," Julie demanded.

"Look, kids, the truth is..." I was interrupted by Julie and Norris as they tried to change the subject.

"The truth is that we were robbed and ransacked," I shouted.

Norris and Julie couldn't believe what they were hearing coming out of my mouth. They were being betrayed by their own father and father-in-law. That was the ultimate betrayal to them. I was going to tell it all. And I was going to blow it.

"What does ransacked mean?" Sadie asked.

"It means that someone totally trashed your house," I replied. "They completely destroyed everything in it."

"Everything?" Sadie asked.

"Yes, everything. They stole all of your mom and dad's valuables. And they broke everything to pieces. They set fire to a lot of things and wrote bad words all over your walls."

Norris and Julie sat there speechless and in shock over my damaging and reckless words.

Sadie started crying hysterically.

"I'm scared."

Michael buried his face in his lap and let out uncontrollable tears as a reaction to his sister crying.

"See what you've done," Julie shouted to me. "You are a mean, angry, and bitter old man."

"You've scared them, and they won't want to ever go back to their house again," Norris shouted with frustration. "They won't ever trust us again because of you."

"They deserve to know the truth."

"Not if it scares and hurts them," Julie shot back.

"Our weekend is ruined," Norris shouted.

Julie and Norris reached to hold and comfort Michael and Sadie. They were furious at me.

Julie turned her face and body away from me with arms folded tightly. With her back to me, she refused to talk to me. She was hurt and felt betrayed. What I had told Michael and Sadie had undermined them. Julie felt foolish and embarrassed that she hadn't told her children the entire truth. But she was angry beyond forgiveness with me.

"You beat all, Dad," Norris said as he shook his head at me. It was quiet. The room felt very cold. I looked the other way in shame, avoiding my son's eyes. I realized that I had done something awful. Suddenly I realized that I had betrayed my son and daughter-in-law in the worst possible way, undermining them in front of their own kids.

Norris broke the silence trying to change the subject.

"I hope you didn't bring your pistol into this hotel."

"No, I didn't."

"I can't believe that you own a gun," Norris reprimanded me.

"It's my second amendment right, thank you," I replied confidently. "Why are you afraid of guns?"

"Because guns kill people."

"Guns don't kill people. People kill people, whether it is with guns, knives, objects, cars, or with their own bare hands like Cain with Abel."

"Well, they should be outlawed because there are a lot of people killed by them."

"There are more people killed by cars than by guns."

"That's impossible."

"No, it's true. I saw the new research in the newspaper that says that 8 out of 100,000 people are killed by guns and 12 out of 100,000 people are killed by car accidents."

"That's a bunch of garbage. How come I didn't see that research? Every day that you turn on the news, you hear of multiple murders with guns."

"You've been listening to too much of the *wacky, crazy left-wing* mainstream media like CBS, NBC, ABC, MSNBC and CNN. They have their hidden agenda and only tell you what they want you to hear."

"Oh, and you think that Fox News is the most accurate of them all? Fox News is the right arm of the Republican party, right-wing nut jobs."

"They are the only news network that is fair and balanced. At least they report all of the news."

"There is nothing fair and balanced about them. They are nothing more than a propaganda machine for the Republican party."

"Believe what you want to believe, Son, but I'm keeping my guns. Do you think that if the government took all guns away that we would be free of crime?"

"Hardly. Criminals can get all the guns they want, and the government can't stop them."

"Let the Feds come for me and my guns. I'll fight them to the end. The government isn't going to take my guns away," I shouted emphatically.

Norris realized that he had been suckered into another

never-ending argument with me.

Norris shook his head in disbelief. He couldn't believe how narrow-minded and opinionated I was. He was kicking himself for allowing himself to be drawn in again to another argument with me.

Its people like Dad who make this country such a dangerous place to live. He is totally brainwashed.

Julie was so angry with me that she had completely tuned me out. It was if I did not exist.

Julie and Norris were disgusted. Julie, Norris, Michael, and Sadie suddenly stood from the table and walked away toward the elevator. They left me standing alone. They were having nothing to do with me. It was as if they had disowned me.

Julie, Norris, and the children took the elevator to their room. Since they were exhausted, they decided to take a nice long nap. They stretched out on their beds, closed their eyes, and shut out the world.

I, thoroughly hurt and insulted, took the elevator to my room and got into bed. I was sulking and pouting. I decided not to speak to Julie or Norris for a good while. But my attitude would soon change when unexpected news would come calling.

CHAPTER NINE

THE CALL

It was about 8 o'clock Friday night. Norris woke from his long nap. He gently shook Julie.

"Julie, wake up."

"Can you believe that we slept this long?" Norris asked.

"What time is it? Julie asked as she stretched her arms and yawned.

Julie was dazed and disoriented by being woken up from a deep sleep. The kids were still asleep.

"8:03," Norris replied.

"Wow."

"Can you believe we slept almost nine hours?"

"Well it sure felt good. We needed it."

They were interrupted by a loud ring of Norris's smart phone.

"Hello."

"This is Hershel," he said in a long drawn out somber tone.

"What's wrong Hershel?"

There was silence on the other end.

"It's about Hilda."

Norris could hear Hershel sobbing.

"Hilda went to be with Jesus about an hour ago."

"Oh, no, I'm so sorry."

Julie tried to listen as she moved her ears close to the phone next to Norris.

"What happened?"

"She had a rough night last night. She never really came out of her unconsciousness after the stroke."

"She is in a much better place now," Hershel continued sobbing profusely over the phone.

"I can't believe that Aunt Hilda is gone, I just can't believe it," Norris shook his head in disbelief.

Julie started sobbing as she reached to hold Norris close in her arms.

"This is so awful and sad," Julie said trying to hold back a flood of tears.

"She went into a cardiac arrest about an hour ago. They tried everything, but they couldn't bring her back," Hershel said with a very somber tone.

"I'm so sorry," Norris tried to comfort Hershel.

Norris set his phone to speakerphone so that Julie could participate in the conversation.

"What are we going to do?" Norris asked.

"There's nothing we can do now. She's with Jesus and the angels," Hershel said with a broken wavering voice.

"Julie and I are so sorry. If there is absolutely anything we can do for you, please, let us know," Norris said with a gentle and sincere voice.

"We'll have to make arrangements pretty soon. I loved her," Hershel cried.

"I know. She loved you too."

"She was a wonderful, kind-hearted, and loving person. She was so generous," Julie said as she remembered all of her fond memories of Aunt Hilda.

"What can we do to help?" Norris asked.

Norris and Julie could hear sobbing coming from Uncle Hershel on the other end.

"You could help by calling and emailing all the family. And it would be greatly appreciated if you could contact all of Hilda's friends."

"Since some of our family members are still together, I thought it might be appropriate to hold a service for her Wednesday afternoon 2 p.m. at the First Church of God," Hershel said.

"Maybe some of the family members could extend their Thanksgiving weekend by a few more days to pay their respects to Hilda."

"I bet most of the family members would stay a little longer to say their final goodbyes," Norris reassured Hershel.

"Yes, I know they would," Julie said. "We love you, Uncle Hershel, and we're so sorry for your loss."

"We will help you in any way we can," Norris replied. "Let us know as soon as you confirm the service time, and I will let everyone know."

"Our thoughts and prayers are with you. We will talk to you later," Julie said compassionately.

As Julie and Norris ended their unexpected conversation with Uncle Hershel, they looked at each other sadly. Julie held Norris closely in her arms as they remained in a long embrace. A long silence filled their room as the children continued sleeping.

Soon Julie and Norris had to break the news to Sadie and Michael. And as much as they didn't want to talk to me, they realized they would have to tell me, too. My reaction to Hilda's unexpected death would be a reaction that would stun everyone. There would be consequences and a price to pay for such cruel words.

CHAPTER TEN

BREAKING THE NEWS

Sadie and Michael were fast asleep snoring in the hotel room. They had been asleep for over nine hours. Julie and Norris were not about to wake them. They had experienced a draining, exhaustive time with the long wait at the ER and then had to face the horrific and traumatic experience with me carelessly explaining every detail of how their house had been totally destroyed.

"We need to tell Louis about Aunt Hilda," Norris said.

"Be my guest," Julie replied. "I'm not going anywhere near that bitter old man. I am so disgusted and angry that I don't care if I ever see him again."

"Surely you don't mean that, sweetheart," Norris replied.

"Read my lips. Oh, yes, I do."

"Okay, I get it, dear. I will go next door and handle this. You just stay here in case the kids wake up and wonder where we are."

Norris gave her a kiss and closed the door behind him.

He stood in front of my hotel room and knocked several times.

There was no answer.

Norris knocked again a little harder than before.

"Dad, are you there?"

Norris knocked again even harder.

"Wake up, Dad, wake up."

Norris shouted so loud that everyone on the fifth floor could hear him.

Without warning I opened my hotel door room slowly and cautiously. I peeked from behind the door.

"Did you miss me? Did I scare you?" I asked sarcastically.

"Cut the crap out, Dad. Can I come in?"

"Well, I suppose."

Norris entered the hotel room.

"Sit down, Dad. I have something important to tell you, and it can't wait."

I pulled up a chair by the bed as Norris sat on the bed. Norris looked directly into my eyes.

"I'm sorry to have to tell you, but Hilda passed away earlier today. Hershel called me less than 30 minutes ago to tell me the news."

The room grew quiet.

"Say something, Dad."

There was a long pause and then I replied.

"So that's the important news you came over here with, banging on my door and waking me up," I said sarcastically.

Norris was stunned. He couldn't believe the words that came out of my mouth.

"Dad, you could at least show some sympathy or say you're sorry."

"Sorry for what?"

"Dad, I can't believe I'm hearing this from you," Norris shook his head in disbelief.

The room grew quiet again.

"Say something, Dad."

"It was her own damn fault that she died. She was wider than the state of Texas," I mocked. "And she was stuffing her face with seconds and thirds faster than the rush of Niagara Falls. She was making all of those God-forsaken noises with her mouth as she stuffed herself."

"Unbelievable," Norris said angrily. "Dad, I can't talk to you anymore. That is the worst thing I've ever heard you say. That is so mean-spirited and doesn't sound like the Christian man I know and love."

"I don't think I'll be attending her funeral. I never could stand the woman," I retorted.

"Unbelievable."

"You heard me. I'm not going to the funeral."

"Have a heart, Dad. It's your own sister, for God's sake. With or without you, her funeral service will be held Wednesday afternoon here in Omaha. And I'm going to pretend I never heard such ugly things come out of your mouth about Hilda."

Norris stood; arms folded in protest, and quickly headed toward the door. Norris slammed the door behind him and left me alone, speechless.

Norris headed back to his room and knocked on the door. Julie greeted him.

"How did it go?"

There was silence between Norris and Julie. Julie could tell by the look on Norris's face that it didn't go well.

Michael and Sadie woke up. They seemed disoriented and dazed. They were half-awake, yawning and stretching every limb of their bodies.

Julie and Norris walked over to hold their children. They held them close. It was quiet. Julie and Norris were waiting for their kids to wake up before telling them the news.

"Kids, kids, wake up," Julie gently coaxed them.

"We have some difficult news to tell you," Norris said.

Julie and Norris's faces looked like statues. No one said a word.

"We lost Aunt Hilda," Julie said with a compassionate voice. There was silence.

"Aunt Hilda went to be with Jesus in heaven today," she continued.

"What, that's not possible. How could that be?" Sadie said trying to understand what her mom had told her.

"She fell into a deep sleep at the hospital and never woke up," Julie continued.

"You mean her heart stopped beating?" Sadie asked.

"Yes, her heart and everything in her body stopped working. She stopped breathing."

"She died?" Sadie asked.

"Yes, she died. God took her away from this Earth to be in heaven with him. We are so sorry to have to tell you this," Norris said.

Sadie broke down and began crying uncontrollably. Michael started crying, too, even though he couldn't completely grasp the meaning of death.

"She was my favorite aunt," Sadie said sadly. "I will really miss her."

"We all will," Julie comforted.

"She was a special aunt and she was always good to you and your brother," Norris agreed. "But we wouldn't want to see her suffer here on Earth and be in all that pain would we?"

"No," Sadie replied.

Julie and Norris held Michael and Sadie in their arms trying to comfort them.

Norris knew it was going to be difficult days ahead for the family and especially for Hershel. Norris was still appalled at my attitude and mean-spiritedness. Norris decided not to tell Julie about all the ugly and hurtful words I said about Hilda.

The Contrary

Norris focused on what was up ahead. He and Julie needed to make a lot of calls to family and friends. And those they couldn't reach by phone, they would email. Norris never liked having to break bad news to anyone and particularly now having to tell everyone about Hilda's death. Still, he had only a short time to let everyone know about the funeral service. He would stay up late and phone everyone. All he could hope for was a better day tomorrow. But that seemed unlikely.

CHAPTER ELEVEN

THE UNEXPECTED VISITOR

Norris stayed up until midnight calling every family member and friend that he could reach. Julie and the kids checked in early and were fast asleep totally exhausted from the day's events. Norris's eyes became heavy and he fell asleep in the chair next to the desk.

Next door in the hotel I was fast asleep in my bed snoring.

All was still and quiet throughout the night until the clocked turned 3:00 a.m.

I thought I was dreaming when I heard a strange, loud womanly voice.

"Louis, wake up," the voice commanded.

I was so sleepy and didn't pay any attention to the voice. I opened my eyes briefly and tried to focus, but I fell back asleep.

I thought it was a dream. I opened my eyes halfway and squinted. My glasses were sitting somewhere near my bed. All I could see was something that resembled a bright light floating above my bed.

"Leave me alone," I groggily said.

The Contrary

"Louis Green, open your eyes and look at me," the voice said a little louder.

I turned over on my side in bed and pulled the covers over my head. I ignored the voice, which was gradually growing louder. The floating light shone more brightly than before.

"Don't pretend you don't see me, Louis. I am real," the voice said clearly.

I buried myself deep under the covers to avoid the light that seemed to grow brighter by the minute.

"That's it! I've had all I can take of you," I shouted at the woman in the light.

"You see, Louis, that's your problem. You've got to get a handle on this before it completely destroys your life," the female voice said emphatically.

"You are a mean, angry, and bitter man, Louis."

"Alright, alright, I hear you," I shouted back as I forced myself out of bed. "Give me a minute to find my glasses."

I was totally annoyed by the woman interrupting my sleep. I didn't have time for such *foolishness*.

I removed all of the covers from around me and was fumbling around searching for my glasses on the nightstand.

"There you are stupid glasses," I shouted as I tried to fit them over my ears.

I sat in bed and focused my eyes. I saw what appeared to be a broad-shouldered woman with large wings all draped in fine white and purple linens. She had curly golden hair and a fair complexion. Her eyes were green, and her arms were stretched out toward me as she spoke. This woman was completely surrounded by a bright light, which also shone on her face and body. She was floating just above my hotel bed.

"Who the hell are you?" I asked angrily.

"I am an angel, and I am not from Hell."

"Yeah right, an angel," I laughed.

"Believe what you want to believe, but I was sent from

Heaven."

"You're from Heaven?"

"Yes, from Heaven. And I am real."

"What do you want from me?"

"I have come here today to help you see how despicable your ways are to Heaven," the angel said with a resounding voice.

"You're calling me despicable? That's a strong word to use don't you think?"

"We are all God's children. Not everyone believes the same way as you do, Louis. Your words are cutting and cause deep strife."

I sat in bed and listened to the woman. I was speechless.

"You hurt everyone you meet or know with your outspoken, hateful words. You are losing your family, and you don't have any more friends. You don't think before you speak. You say anything you feel like saying without considering the feelings of others."

"I do?" Louis asked.

"Come on, Louis, who do you think you are fooling? As an angel, I see everything. I have seen all of the despicable acts you have committed against your brothers and sisters. God is not happy with you. Still God loves you no matter what you do. But you must change your ways, Louis. You need to change your heart. You need unconditional love."

Louis shook his head in disbelief.

"How do I know that you are real and not just a dream?"

"Louis, you are wide awake right now, and you have your glasses on. You see me floating above your bed, and we are having this conversation about your attitude on life. What more do you need from me to know that I am real? If you don't change your ways soon something awful will force you to change. Then you will have no choice. Take heed to what I say. Take heed to what I say. Take heed," the angel's voice began to fade as the bright light started to dim. I sat there with amazement and disbelief. I continued to stare at the angel as she gradually faded away. After several minutes, the angel had completely disappeared. I shook my head and thought it was all one bad dream. I laughed to myself at such foolishness of angels visiting me in my hotel room. I took my glasses off and placed them on the nightstand. I fell into a deep sleep until the rays of the sunrise crept through my window and woke me up.

What a crazy dream I had last night. It seemed so real, but it couldn't be true.

I decided to keep the angel visitation to myself. People would think I was losing my mind if I told them all that had happened last night—a woman with wings who talked to me claiming to be an angel. I decided to chalk it up to a wild and crazy dream. I would go on with my life as if nothing had ever happened. I decided I would continue to stay the same old Louis. Yet my decision would result in harsh consequences in the not-too-distant future.

CHAPTER TWELVE

BREAKFAST WITH THE FAMILY

I rolled out of my bed yawning and stretching. It was almost 9 a.m. Saturday morning. I took a shower and got dressed.

I left my hotel room and knocked on the door of my son's room.

No one answered.

I knocked loudly several times.

Norris stumbled to the door.

"We're trying to get some sleep around here, Dad."

"I'm hungry, and it's time to eat. I'd like to join you all for breakfast," I replied.

"Why don't you go and get yourself something to eat. I'll be there in a little bit. I'm just waking up, okay?"

I honored my son's request and took the elevator down to the first floor where breakfast was being served.

I helped myself to a large plate of grits, hash brown potatoes, eggs, bacon, and toast. I found a table in the corner away from the other hotel guests. I helped myself to orange juice and some strong black coffee.

I took a bite of my toast. I read the newspaper, which I called the *liberal rag* and sipped my coffee.

I was used to critiquing every single news article from top to bottom. I waited a long time. Norris and his family hadn't come down yet.

I was growing impatient waiting on them to join me for breakfast. I had finished my second cup of coffee, downed two eggs, grits, and my last strip of bacon. Finally, Norris arrived.

"Sorry it took so long, Dad. Julie and the kids couldn't make it. They are sleeping in. They are totally exhausted."

I knew that was a pitiful excuse. I knew that those words were code for *I can't stand your guts. I don't want be around you.*

Norris filled his plate with eggs, bacon, toast, and hash brown potatoes. He sat by me and sipped some orange juice.

I was quiet and didn't say another word.

"Is there something wrong, Dad?"

There was complete silence.

"Dad, what's wrong. Say something."

I kept staring at my plate.

"Dad, I made a special effort to join you for breakfast. If you're pissed at me, let me know. But at least speak to me like a cordial human being."

Again there was silence.

"Okay, if you're not going to be civil to me, I'm going to get up right now and leave."

I stared at Norris as if to speak. My eyes looked like I had seen a resurrected body and my faced looked perplexed.

"You're scaring me, Dad. You look strange."

"I don't want to talk about it."

"What happened? Are you still stewing about the fights we had about all that political stuff?"

"No, although I've haven't forgiven you yet."

"Is it about all the things Julie said about you?"

"No, although I still haven't forgiven her either." I pouted.
"Then, good Lord, what is it, Dad? Tell me. Please tell me."
I was very still and quiet.
"Okay, Dad, if you're not going to tell me, I'm going to head back to my hotel room."

I couldn't stand the annoying persistence of my son trying to pry the words from my mouth. I swore I wouldn't tell anyone about what happened last night for fear of looking foolish. And it would look like I had lost my mind. I was not ready for anyone to send me to a home that was full of people with dementia and Alzheimer's disease.

"Okay, okay, here's what I am bummed out about," I said sounding discouraged. "I didn't want to tell you about last night for fear that you might think I am crazy."

"You don't have to tell me you're crazy. I already know you're crazy."

"See. There you go talking about me being crazy."

"Dad, you know I'm just joking with you."

"Well, it's not funny."

"Sorry. So what happened last night that you don't want to talk about?"

"Well, there was a woman who visited me in my room last night. Not just any ole' woman."

"Dad, I didn't think you were fooling around with other women after mom died."

"I'm not, I mean, I don't. She wasn't a real woman."

Norris was puzzled as to what I was trying to say. His eyes looked intrigued and his mouth was wide open.

"What do you mean, she wasn't a real woman?"

"She said she was an angel."

"You mean one of those Victoria Secret lingerie angels?"

Norris jokingly replied.

"Of course not Son. I heard this woman's voice. It was loud and woke me up at 3 a.m."

"Where was she in your hotel room?"

"She was floating over my bed in a bright pillar of light."

"Yeah right, she was floating over your bed," Norris replied as if he didn't believe me.

"Yes, she was floating over my bed. I tried to cover my face and fall back to sleep thinking it was one bad dream, but she kept bugging me saying, *'get up, Louis, get up, Louis'*."

Finally I was so annoyed that I fumbled around looking for my stupid glasses to see who she really was. I found my glasses, and I focused my eyes on the bright light over my bed. I saw this woman with large wings looking right at me and mouthing words. I told her that she wasn't real, that I was just dreaming. She showed me how real she was through shining a blinding light. She said she was from heaven and that she was an angel."

Norris laughed loudly. Everyone eating in the breakfast area stopped what they were doing and stared strangely at Norris.

"Get real, Dad. It was all a dream. Don't believe everything you see or hear," Norris said sarcastically.

"I told her that she was just a dream. But she kept on telling me how real she was and that she was definitely an angel."

"I've heard everything, Dad. What did your angel tell you?" Norris mocked.

"She told me that I was a bitter, angry man."

"Well, Dad, we all know that. It doesn't take an angel to tell you that," Norris joked.

"There you go, making fun of me. The angel said that I needed to change my ways and that I was too critical and judgmental of people".

"You, critical and judgmental? No way," Norris laughed.

"She said that I have hurt everyone that I have come into contact with."

"You don't say," Norris replied flippantly.

"She said something awful was going to happen to me if I didn't change my ways."

"What do you think is going to happen to you? You'll be eaten by a little green monster?"

"There you go again, Son, making fun of me," I disapproved.

"Surely you don't believe that garbage," Norris replied. "It was a really bad dream that seemed life-like. It is true that we put up with a lot of things about you that we don't like. But we still love you, Dad. I wouldn't pay any attention to that dream other than it would be nice for you to be kind to others sometimes. Well, Dad, I'm going to head upstairs to check on Julie and the kids. Everything will be okay. Next time you'll have better dreams than this one."

"See you later, Son."

Norris took the elevator to the fifth floor and walked to his hotel room. He slipped his hotel card into the door and unlocked it. Julie and the kids were still sleeping. He sat by the desk and checked his email on his phone. He pondered about what I had told him about my angelic visit. He thought about how crazy my dream was. He thought that maybe I was having some kind of an awakening experience or a hallucination. Nevertheless, Norris was glad that I had shared my dream with him.

CHAPTER THIRTEEN

A CALL TO THE POLICE STATION

As Norris sat checking his email, Julie and the kids awoke.

"Ahh," Sadie took a long and loud yawn.

"Wow, that was some good sleep," Julie said as she stretched out her arms and legs.

Michael was mumbling under his breath about being hungry. It was about 10:30 a.m. on Saturday morning.

"Hope you got plenty of sleep," Norris said to them.

"Did you get any sleep?" Julie asked.

"Yes, I got some. I was downstairs eating breakfast and talking to Dad."

There was silence as if Norris had said a bad word or had said something wrong. No one replied because no one in that room liked me. Norris was the only one who could tolerate me.

"They stopped serving breakfast at 10," Norris continued. "But we can go grab lunch somewhere if you'd like."

"We'll get showered and dressed," Julie replied.

"Okay, I'll be waiting here."

Before they could say another word, there was a loud ring on Norris's smart phone.

"Hello."

"Is this Norris Green?" the man asked from the other end.

"You're speaking to him."

"This is Detective Riley from the Omaha Police Department. I need you to come down to the main station right away."

"Why, Detective Riley, what's going on?"

"We've found the scumbag who did it."

"You mean that lowlife schmuck that trashed our house?"

"Yes, we found him, and he confessed to it all."

"Unbelievable. Great fast work, Detective Riley."

"I'll need your wife and your father to come down to the station, too."

"I'll get my wife, the kids, and my dad. We'll be down there shortly. Thank you, Officer, for catching that no good scumbag."

Norris fumed as the memory of his ransacked house came back to him. Detective Riley's call conjured up the painful memories of coming home to that trashed house early yesterday morning. He couldn't wait to confront the person who wrecked his house and his life. He had some choice words saved to unload on that person. Norris pondered in his mind what his visit to the police station would be like as he patiently waited for his wife and children to finish getting ready.

I'm going to choke that bastard.

Norris wondered what he looked like and how he acted. Norris wondered why he had done such a reprehensible act and what his motive was.

"Honey, we're ready," Julie tried to get his attention. "Earth to Norris."

"Oh, yeah, sorry about that," Norris replied as he returned to reality.

"Are we going to lunch or not?" she asked.

"Change of plans. We're going to the police station."

"Why are we going there?"

"To meet the moron who totally destroyed our home."

"You mean they've already found the person who did it? That's some fast detective work. But this is going to be a long day. What do we do with the kids while we're at the police station?"

"Maybe they can sit out in the lobby and play their video games. Sadie can watch Michael," Norris replied.

"Are we going to have to sit around all day long at the police station, Dad?" Sadie asked.

"It won't take long," Norris promised.

"That's what you said when we sat around the hospital for like three days," Sadie said dramatically.

"Three days my foot, it was more like 14 hours," Norris replied.

"That's our drama queen," Julie interjected with confidence.

Sadie pretended to ignore them.

"I'm starving," she said.

"Me too," Michael said.

"Let's make a run through McDonald's and get something to go," Julie suggested.

"Okay," Sadie said.

"Yeah, I want a Happy Meal," Michael replied.

The Green family locked their hotel room. Norris left a note under my door telling me to meet them at the Omaha Police Station. Norris and his family headed toward the elevator. They took it down to the ground floor. Then they left the hotel parking lot in their car. They drove east toward downtown Omaha.

"There's a McDonalds." Sadie shouted.

The Green family pulled up to the drive-thru window and ordered their lunch.

Meanwhile I found the note that my son left. I was dumbfounded.

The note read: *Meet us at the downtown police station ASAP:*

505 South 15th Street.

After reading my son's note, I locked my hotel room and headed toward the elevator. I started my truck and headed toward downtown.

Norris and Julie ate their McDonald's lunch with the kids on the way to the police station. Norris was preoccupied and didn't say much while he drove. All he could think of was how the encounter at the station would go. He thought about who the perpetrator might be and what his motive was for ransacking and robbing their beautiful home. He thought about what he would say to the sick person who cut their cat into pieces. He was at a loss for words as to what to say. He was still angry about the whole incident and wasn't sure how to handle it.

Norris and Julie finally arrived at the police station after their 15-minute drive from the hotel. They had gulped down their meal from McDonalds and were searching for a parking spot. They found an open parking space on the street about a block away from the police station.

The Green family parked their car and got out.

"Please grab all of your trash from lunch, so we can properly dispose of it," Norris requested.

"Okay, Dad. You don't have to say it again," Sadie replied reluctantly.

Everyone grabbed their McDonalds bags and tossed them into a nearby garbage container on the street.

The Green family walked a short block and entered the Omaha Police Station. They approached a police officer sitting at the front desk. He was sturdy and muscular. The officer looked like a former Marine sergeant.

"We are here to see Detective Riley," Norris said.

"Who are you?" the desk officer asked.

"I am Norris Green, and this is my family."

"State your business as to why you are here."

"We are here about the case of my house being ransacked

and robbed."

"Let me see. Are you located at 2126 Cedar Point Road? Oh yes, I see. We caught the guy who did it. Just wait here in the lobby and Detective Riley will be here shortly."

The Green family took their seats in the lobby and stretched their legs out to relax. This was the last place Sadie and Michael wanted to be spending their Saturday. Sadie and Michael sat slouched in their seats with their hands cupped under their chins. Boredom was about to set in.

Meanwhile, I was circling the block of the police station looking for a parking space. I had cursed every driver that was in my way. Finally I found a free parking spot on the street about two blocks away from the station.

I got out of my truck and sprinted toward the station. Before I approached the traffic light across the street from the station, I was solicited by a grungy looking old man. The man had teeth missing and looked like he hadn't taken a bath in years. His body reeked with cheap alcohol, and he was dressed in rags. His whole face was covered in hair from not shaving or grooming.

"Could you help this old vet out?" The old man asked as he held his hand out.

"Veteran my foot," I yelled. "You're no vet. You look like you crawled out of the sewer."

"I proudly served in the Vietnam War."

"Well, look at you now, you're nothing but a drunk and a worthless piece of crap."

The old man ignored my harsh words. His mind was on getting some help from me.

"Look, I'm starving, could you help me out with a bill or two?"

"So I can support your alcohol habit? Why don't you go down to the local shelter and get some help. That's what they're there for."

"Come on; help out a brother in need."

The homeless man had a small fire going in a make-shift grill that he had made. It appeared he had built the fire to stay warm and possibly to cook anything that was edible.

"I'm so hungry I could throw you on the grill and eat you," the homeless man shouted.

I was troubled and angered at the old man's remarks. I turned my back and walked away.

"I'm just kidding. It was a joke," the man tried to reassure me.

I didn't take the remark kindly. I was fuming mad.

"That's the trouble with this country. All of you freeloaders and moochers living on food stamps and welfare are draining us taxpayers. Get a job."

"I can't get any work. There are no jobs out there for me."

"Have you tried looking?"

"Come on, help out a brother," the man persistently begged.

I was disgusted and annoyed by the behavior of the homeless man. I didn't have time to waste with a bum. I needed to be at the police station about 15 minutes ago. I threw a wadded up dollar bill at the old man.

"Here, take this for your bottle of Thunderbird," I shouted.

The homeless man was insulted and had about all he could take.

"I don't want your stinking dollar. You can take old George and wipe your ass with it," he chastised.

I was very angry at this point. I started shouting at the old man.

"You ungrateful, son of a bitch. All you want to do is rip off upstanding law-abiding citizens like me."

I coughed up a big wad of saliva and spit it at the old homeless man. Then I turned my back to the man and walked away. The homeless man stood there speechless in disbelief. He had never had anyone treat him so vile and with such contempt as I had treated him. He could see the fire in my eyes and the venom spewing out of me. I am sure that he thought to himself that all I needed was a pitchfork and I would be complete.

I wasted no time or words with that man. I was fed up with lowlife people ripping upstanding law-abiding citizens off and stealing from the government and the taxpayers.

I opened the front door to the police station still trying to calm down from losing my temper with the old man. I approached the main desk at the station.

"Yes?" the desk officer asked.

"I'm here for Officer Riley," I said hurriedly still trying to catch my breath.

"You mean *Detective* Riley. And who are you?"

"I am Louis Green. I am Norris Green's father."

"State your business."

"I am here as a witness to the ransacking case of the Green home."

"You mean the one at 2126 Cedar Point Road?"

"Yes, that's the one."

"Take a seat over there in the lobby. Detective Riley will be out shortly."

I stepped around the corner of the hallway and found the lobby.

"You finally made it," Norris said as he caught a glimpse of my face.

"Yes, finally," I said grumpily. "This old homeless guy wasted my time begging for money."

"You see plenty of those around here in downtown Omaha. You get used to that. It's a shame how the city has treated them. The police are always running these people off claiming that it is bad for tourism."

"I'm glad. The city can run them off anytime they want to. They are a menace to society."

"There you go again, Dad, being heartless and mean-spirited. The homeless need our help."

"Now you're the one that's gullible and a sucker. Those people are freeloaders and moochers. They need to get jobs."

"They can't help themselves. They've lost their homes, jobs, and families. We need to help them get back on their feet again."

"They are drunks and addicts—worthless pieces of crap."

"We just need to help them. We need to feed them and get them off the streets into a home of some kind."

"You're a bleeding-heart liberal for believing such crap about those worthless homeless people. They can't be helped, and they don't want to be helped. It says in the *Bible* that the poor will always be with us. And they are one of the reasons our taxes keep going up higher and higher."

"If you all are going to continue your ranting immature antics acting like two-year-olds, I am going to leave. I'm going to take the kids with me back to the hotel," Julie said disgustingly.

"I'm sorry, Julie," Norris apologized.

"I'm not. I meant every word that I said," I meanly replied. "I'll speak when I damn well want to."

There was a long period of silence where no one spoke or looked at each other. It was good that it was a Saturday and there was no one else waiting in the lobby except the Green family. It's a wonder that the police officers didn't escort Norris and me out of the building considering how loud and disorderly we were. Norris and I had made another awful and miserable scene.

The long silence was broken when Detective Riley entered the lobby.

"You must be the Green family."

"Yes, I'm Norris, and this is my wife Julie and these are my children, Sadie and Michael. Oh, and this is my dad, Louis." He was still angry at me for making a scene.

The Contrary

"Good to meet you all," Detective Riley said in a dry monotone voice. "In a minute we are going back to the interrogation room. You are going to meet the suspect that ransacked and robbed your home. It is best that you stay calm and not get emotional about the crime. We caught him in the act of ransacking another house last night. We cuffed him and took him down to headquarters. We booked him and then we got him to talking."

Detective Riley had a low deep voice that reminded you of the deep bass note drone you hear when bagpipes are playing.

"He knew he was caught red-handed last night ransacking that house, but we didn't know that he would confess to the crime he committed against you."

"Wow, great work, Detective Riley," Norris said with excitement.

"Follow me and take a left at the first door."

Norris, Julie and I followed Detective Riley down the long corridor and entered the first door on the left behind the officer.

We entered the large rectangular room. There was nothing but a few chairs and a long wooden table with some microphones attached to it. There were security cameras at each corner of the room. Norris and Julie stared intently around the room at the bareness of it all. There was a glass booth with a window behind the table where the detectives could view the suspects being interrogated. It was just like the scene you see on those *CSI* television shows.

"I'll bring him in shortly. Remember to get a handle on your emotions. You are here to face the suspect and to ask any questions you might have. Then we will need you to file charges through an official police report," Detective Riley explained.

"What will they do to him?" Norris asked

"You mean fines and sentences?"

"Yes, like will he have to do jail time?"

"It's most likely that he will. It really depends on who he

gets as a judge and if this is his first offense or not."

"If he gets a look at our faces, could he commit an act of revenge against us for pressing charges?" Julie asked.

"It's possible but highly unlikely."

"Why is that?"

"First of all, he will be held without bond in this jail because no one has stepped forward to post bond. Secondly, he probably won't get off easy. He will serve some jail time."

"But he knows where we live," Julie said hesitantly.

"True, but I wouldn't worry about it. We are here to protect you in case that should happen. If necessary, we will park our squad cars in front of your house with 24-hour monitoring if that makes you feel better," he continued in his dry monotone voice. "Wait here and we'll bring him in."

Norris, Julie, and I sat there in that naked room and looked at each other. I thought about the kind of person who would commit such a senseless act. I pictured in my mind the sick, demented *animal* that the suspect would look like. The clock ticked loudly above the overwhelming silence. No one entered the room. The suspense was too much. The anticipation continued to grow minute by minute. We sat on the edge of our seats waiting for the door to open.

The silence was broken when the door opened loudly. In came Detective Riley with the other officers and the suspect handcuffed with his head held down low. Norris, Julie and, I couldn't see his face at first because it was hidden by his chest. All we could see was a body with long dark hair. The man was wearing an old torn shirt and ragged jeans. Norris and Julie noticed that he was wearing familiar looking army boots, but they couldn't remember where they had seen him.

The suspect looked up. At first all we could see was a face with a goatee and wire-rimmed glasses. Then everyone got still and quiet. Norris's face was filled with shock. He looked as though he had seen a ghost. Hysteria and distress were written all over Julie's face. My face was flushed with a deep beet-red color. There was rage and anger written all over my face.

We couldn't believe our eyes. The suspect was one of our family members, my nephew of all people. To Norris and Julie that seemed incomprehensible. But it wasn't to me. I couldn't take it anymore.

"You sick demented animal," I shouted in a fit of rage as I stood and shook my fist.

"Dad, sit down and shut up," Norris shouted.

The officers helped constrain me as I was ready to strangle the suspect.

"We've got a mess on our hands," Julie said with confusion as she realized who the suspect was.

Norris looked into his eyes. It was like he was looking into his own eyes through a mirror. He couldn't believe that the suspect who confessed was my nephew Adrian.

"Are you sure you have the right one?" Norris asked Detective Riley.

"Positive. He confessed the whole thing, and we've got it on video. We've even got a signed statement from him on file. What more proof do you need?"

"This is just too hard to believe," Julie said.

Adrian remained silent with a blank stare. His face didn't show any emotion even when I tongue-lashed him severely.

"Why did you do it, Adrian? Why did you trash our home?" Julie asked.

Adrian refused to look at any of us. He remained silent.

"We're family, Adrian. Family doesn't do this to each other," Julie said emotionally.

There was still no response from Adrian. He looked the other way and pretended not to hear her.

After seeing that we were getting nowhere, we sat silently in our chairs seething over the situation with frustration.

"He was probably advised to remain silent since anything he

says can be used against him in court," Detective Riley said. "We need you to sign this statement pressing charges against Adrian."

There was a long pause as Norris and Julie thought about what to do. They were totally disgusted at Adrian for destroying their house and angry at Adrian for killing their cat, but they weren't ready to press charges against one of their family members, a nephew of all people.

"Let's get this bastard put away for life. Give him the electric chair," I shouted again in a fit of rage.

There was silence and reluctance again from Norris and Julie.

"What's wrong with you bleeding-heart liberals? You're always coddling the criminals."

Julie and Norris thought of the awful life Adrian had been exposed to. He was raised by a single mother who worked hard to hold down two minimum-wage jobs. In his younger days, Adrian was always getting into trouble by stealing or vandalizing. They felt sorry for him and his life. They were so glad to hear that he had discovered art as a teenager and that he had been accepted into art school in St. Louis. They felt there was hope for Adrian and that he was finally doing something positive with his life. Maybe he could turn his life around. Then this terrible incident had to happen. They were caught in a miserable dilemma. If they pressed charges against their own family member, it might destroy his life for good. He would be sentenced to jail time and be given a hefty fine. And he would carry another police record, which would be considered a felony, making it difficult to get hired anywhere for work.

"Nail the bastard," I blurted out. "He deserves everything that's coming to him. That's the trouble with you wishy-washy bleeding-heart liberals. You give them a slap on the wrist, and they're back on the streets again doing the same crime. The police catch them, arrest them, and then the bleeding-heart

The Contrary

liberal judges let the criminals walk the streets. They're doing nothing but promoting crime. Those lily-livered judges and this liberal good-for-nothing political system we have. Why have laws on the books if you don't enforce them?"

"Detective Riley, could my husband and I have a private moment together to discuss what to do?" Julie interrupted.

"What is there to discuss? There's nothing to discuss. He committed the crime, he does the time," I mocked Julie.

"Yes, I'll give you a few minutes by yourselves," the detective replied.

Julie and Norris left the room and stood by each other in the long hallway outside the interrogation room.

I sat there frustrated with Norris and Julie. I had all the foolishness and liberalism that I could take from my son and daughter-in-law. I was ready to leave.

"How do you feel about all of this?" Julie asked.

"I'm torn. It just breaks my heart."

"It breaks my heart too. This shouldn't have ever happened, particularly from our own family member."

"You're right, but it did."

"So what should we do?"

Norris paused.

"I think we shouldn't press charges. I know you're probably surprised by my answer after all of the damage and destruction that he did to our home. But he's really pitiful considering the way he was raised."

"Don't forget he killed our cat," Julie interrupted.

"Yes, I know and it is very wrong. We have been deeply hurt by all of this. But if we are going to be kind, loving human beings, we also need to be forgiving. We need to love people unconditionally."

"But it's so hard to forgive someone for doing such a horrible thing."

"You're right. It's hard for me, too. But it is Adrian we are talking about. If we press charges against him, we could damage him for life. Instead, maybe we can suggest that he be placed on probation and do some community service. And maybe he can get some therapy somewhere."

"Okay, so you're saying we should drop the charges?"

"Yes, that's what I'm saying, sweetheart."

Julie bit her lip and held it tightly. She disagreed with Norris and his decision, but she was tired of arguing about the whole thing. She wanted to get their lives put back together again. She dreamed of getting their home cleaned and restored to its original state so that they could move back in.

"Okay, let's tell the detective we've decided not to charge him," Julie said.

Julie and Norris knocked on the door and Detective Riley greeted them.

They sat down to listen to Julie and Norris's decision.

"We've decided not to press charges against our family member Adrian with the provision that he serve 1000 hours of community service and get some psychiatric counseling," Norris said emphatically.

"What? Are you crazy? You're going to let this animal go scot-free?" I objected.

"Yes. We've decided to give him another chance," Julie replied.

"Detective is it possible that Adrian could do community service like we suggested and seek help for anger management?" she asked.

"Well, first of all, I think you're making a big mistake by not pressing charges," Detective Riley commented in his monotone voice.

"You tell 'em, Detective," I shouted.

"If you don't press charges, it still won't keep him from possibly going to jail. Remember, he was caught red-handed ransacking and stealing from another house last night. But it is your choice to make."

"We won't have any part in sending Adrian to jail," Norris replied.

"Is that your final decision?" the detective asked.

"Yes," Norris and Julie said the word almost simultaneously.

"You fools, you *gullible* liberal fools," I judged. "This will surely come back to bite you. You will regret this for the rest of your lives."

"It's their decision, Louis."

Detective Riley stood from his chair as Julie and Norris stood. I remained seated. Detective Riley reached out his hand to shake theirs.

"Thank you for stopping by."

"Thank you for respecting our decision," Norris replied.

Before they left the room, Julie and Norris patted Adrian on the shoulder.

"We understand. Everything's going to be okay," they tried to reassure him.

I was so upset and angry with Norris and Julie that I stared into space as I remained seated in my chair in the interrogation room. I let them leave the room. I thought about what a bad decision Norris and Julie had made.

"Fools, *naïve fools*," I mocked Norris and Julie after they left. I continued to shake my head in disbelief.

Norris and Julie beckoned their children Sadie and Michael to leave with them so they could head back to their hotel room.

They were tired and disgusted with how the whole scenario had turned out. Yet, they were relieved that they were not responsible for ruining Adrian's life and sending him to jail. They didn't care what I thought about the whole thing. To them, I was a narrow-minded bigot who spewed venom.

I didn't want to be around Norris and Julie for a very long time. I didn't want to have anything to do with people who coddled criminals. I felt what Norris and Julie had done was a crime in itself.

Finally, I stood from my chair and shook Detective Riley's hand. I left the station and walked the two blocks to my truck and then headed back to my hotel room. I was angry, tired, and disgusted. I felt like I had lost a major battle. I was down and depressed. I decided not to talk to Norris or Julie for a while. I would go straight to bed and sleep the whole nightmare off. Tomorrow, I promised, would be a better day. But boy how wrong I was.

CHAPTER FOURTEEN

TAKE HEED

I parked my truck outside the Holiday Inn. I took the elevator to the fifth floor and unlocked my door. Without brushing my teeth or changing clothes, I plopped onto the bed from exhaustion. I was sure that Norris, Julie, and the kids had already arrived in their room and had gone to bed. I turned the lights off in my room and fell into a deep sleep.

I slept peacefully and tuned the world out. I dreamed about my memorable times with my wife Samantha. I was sitting with her in a field of daisies laughing and enjoying a picnic lunch. She looked so pretty in her blue sundress with her hair blowing in the wind. It was an unforgettable time. In those days, I was happy. I missed her very much. I wished I could get those happy days back again. I was tired of feeling angry at the world. Why couldn't I just feel good again? Why couldn't I be happy again?

My beautiful peaceful dream was interrupted by a loud voice calling my name. It was 3 a.m.

"Louis, wake up," the voice demanded.

I was so exhausted that I fell back to sleep.

A bright blinding light filled my entire hotel room like when the sun is at high noon. Everything in my room lit up. It was so bright that I couldn't ignore it. I pulled my bed covers over my head and buried myself deep inside. But no matter how hard I tried to shut my eyes and keep the light out, I was unsuccessful. The light was piercing and actually hurt my eyes.

"Louis, if you don't get up this very minute I'm going to turn the light up brighter so that you won't be able to stand it any longer."

I recognized the voice as the woman's voice who claimed to be an angel.

I was agitated from being interrupted by the blinding light and the woman's piercing voice. My blood boiled, and I had all I could take from this angel.

I threw my covers on the floor and sat in my bed at attention. I stared at an object floating above my bed accentuated by the bright blinding light.

I reached over to my nightstand and searched for my glasses. I accidentally pushed several items to the floor including my wallet and keys. Finally I found my glasses and put them on. I focused my eyes on the large object floating above my bed.

"It's you again," I said sarcastically.

"Yes, it's me."

"Look, you don't exist. You're not real. You're part of a dream, part of my imagination. I'm just having a bad dream," I said trying to reason with what my eyes were seeing.

"Go ahead and tell yourself that if it makes you feel better," the angel replied as I put my fingers in my ears so that I didn't have to hear her voice.

"We've got to talk," the angel demanded.

"Leave me alone."

"Not a chance."

"I refuse to believe you are real. I need to get therapy to

work this one out."

"You don't need therapy, you need God. Take a deep breath, calm down, and talk to me like I'm real because I am definitely real."

I took several deep breaths. I started to calm down and appeared to be in a better frame of mind than before.

"Okay, angel or whatever you are, I'm all ears."

"I'm not sure what I need to do to get your attention, Louis. You just don't get it. I tried to tell you the other night how mean and bitter you are, but you didn't listen. Today was a good example of that. You were very rude to that homeless man when he asked you for help."

"But, but...." I tried to finish.

"How do you know you weren't talking to Jesus today when he asked you for some help?" the angel asked.

"Because he wasn't Jesus, he was some old worthless drunk."

"There you go, Louis. You have no love in your heart. And what makes you so sure you weren't talking to Jesus?"

"Cause Jesus doesn't look and behave like that."

"Well, you could have easily been talking to him. How does that make you feel knowing you could have been talking to the King of Kings?"

I became speechless.

"Then today you treated Norris and Julie with contempt and disrespect because you didn't agree with them. They are your family. We are committed to love our neighbors as ourselves even if we don't always like someone or agree. And about Adrian, what you said to him was disgraceful."

"He's not family. He's a sick animal. He had that coming to him. He deserved it for that despicable act he committed against Norris and Julie."

"Now, Louis, you don't have any right to judge. God's the only one that can rightfully judge. You don't know Adrian's heart and all that he's been through. God can forgive each and every one of us for detestable and despicable acts that we commit. There is hope for Adrian."

"Hope my foot."

"Well, then, you don't know God very well. God can make the impossible possible. The best thing you can do for Adrian is to pray for him and try to help him."

"But, but…." I said trying to defend myself.

"You can't talk your way out of this one. There is hope for you too, Louis. God can change your heart, but you have to be willing to change. Right now I sense you aren't willing because of your spiteful, mean-spirited, self-righteous, and judgmental attitude. It's going to take a whole lot of work with you to get you to change. I think you're going to have to learn it the hard way. You're going to have to learn it on your own because you're hard-headed, hard-hearted, and not willing to change. You are on the pathway to destruction with the way you are treating others."

I continued to listen.

"Don't make me have to come down again from Heaven to warn you. If you don't change your ways soon, you will be changed by something catastrophic that will happen in your life. Time is running out for you, Louis. God loves you very much but is saddened by your mean-spirited, hateful ways. I need to start seeing changes in the way you treat others here on Earth. You could start by apologizing to Norris and Julie and asking them to forgive you."

"Ask them to forgive me for what? I didn't do anything wrong."

"Don't start again with me, Louis. You haven't listened to a word I've said. You can't win this argument.

"Take heed, Louis, take heed," the angel's voice became

softer as she started to fade into the distance.

"Take heed, take heed," the angel said as she completely disappeared.

I was dumbfounded and exhausted. I couldn't believe that I had wasted my time and sleep talking to an imaginary voice and vision. Again, I believed that it was all one bad nightmare. I decided to place my glasses on the nightstand and retrieve the covers from the floor. I placed the covers and comforter over my body and placed my pillows under my head. I decided not to pay any attention to the *crazy dream* and *figment of my imagination*. I was going to be my comfortable old self. If no one liked me because of who I was, I didn't care. It was already 4:30 a.m. I fell back into a deep sleep again. Little did I know that my fate was about to change.

CHAPTER FIFTEEN

THE MORNING AFTER

It was almost 7 a.m. Sunday morning when I awoke from my awful angelic dream. I considered it more of a nightmare than an actual dream. The sunlight was piecing through the window almost blinding my eyes. I stretched and yawned while still sitting in bed. I reached over to the night stand to find my glasses and placed them gently over my eyes and ears. I focused my eyes and looked around the room. There was no angelic woman with large wings and no blinding bright light other than the sun shining through my window. I shook my head in disbelief when I thought about my *crazy dream*. I was still very tired from being rudely awakened by some woman claiming to be an angel. Thoughts ran through my mind about all of the things that she told me. I really needed to talk to someone about my angelic experience but didn't want anyone to think I was crazy. I thought about calling my son Norris or knocking on Norris and Julie's hotel room door. But it was early, and they were probably still asleep. I thought that Norris and Julie wouldn't want to spend any time with me after our angry disagreement at the police station. I thought about asking

The Contrary

Norris to have breakfast with me downstairs so I could tell him everything that happened last night, but I realized Norris was fed up with me and would not want to hear another angel story and would only think that I had lost my mind.

So I got out of bed and immediately took a shower. I dried myself off and got dressed in yesterday's shirt and khaki pants. I shaved and brushed my hair and teeth. I put on my dark blue loafers and opened my hotel room door. I locked the door behind me and headed down the hall to the elevator. I unlocked my truck, started it up, and headed toward downtown. I was hungry and decided to stop at the neighborhood Waffle House for breakfast. I thought it was wise to give Norris and Julie some space and time to themselves.

I pulled into the parking lot of the Waffle House. As I stepped out of my truck, I could smell the bacon and waffles permeating the air. I opened the door to the restaurant and was greeted by the hostess. She asked me how many were in my party. I told her that it was just me. The Waffle House was very crowded. The tables were filled with families and church-goers trying to eat breakfast before the early services. Since it was so crowded, the hostess seated me at the counter where I could see the cook preparing breakfast. I sat on the bar stool and a waitress appeared.

"Will you have coffee or juice?" the waitress asked.

"Give me coffee, black."

"No cream or sugar?"

"No, I just want coffee, black."

I whistled to myself and appeared bored. There was a gentleman sitting next to me who tried to strike up a conversation.

"It's a beautiful morning," the man said to me.

"Yes, if you say so."

"Well, God made it, so it is a beautiful morning."

"Never mind me. I've had a terrible night," Louis replied.

"Do you want to talk about it?"

"You wouldn't understand. You'd probably think I was losing my mind if I told you."

"Try me. My name is Charlie," the man said as he extended his hand out to me.

I didn't know what to think. I was about to talk to a stranger in Omaha. I didn't know anyone in Omaha except my son and daughter-in-law. But I really felt like I needed to talk to someone about what had happened. I wasn't sure if I should tell it to a stranger. Then I thought it over again. Maybe I should tell my story to a stranger because I would never see this man again and there would be no gossip. Maybe the stranger wouldn't judge me or think that I was crazy. I decided to talk to him.

"My name is Louis. I'm visiting my son and daughter-in-law for Thanksgiving."

"Where are you from?"

"You wouldn't have ever heard of it. It's such a small town."

"Try me."

"Griswold, Iowa," I said proudly.

"Actually, I know the town. My cousin lives there."

"Who's your cousin?"

"Tom Kildare."

"I know him. He used to work at the local factory. Too bad they shut the factory down and let everyone go."

"Yes, it is too bad."

"What's he doing now?"

"He's selling insurance for State Farm."

I paused and thought about whether it was wise to tell my story to Charlie since Griswold was a small town. Charlie could start talking about it and tell his cousin. Next thing you know, it could be all over town. But Charlie was friendly and seemed trustworthy. Charlie seemed like the kind of guy you could tell anything to, like an older brother. I decided to tell it all.

"Look, Charlie, if I tell you what happened to me last night, will you promise not to judge me or think that I've lost my mind?"

"I promise to never say a word about this."

I let out a sigh of relief, let my guard down, and started to feel comfortable around Charlie.

"Okay, here goes nothing."

"Sorry to interrupt you, but are you ready to order?" the waitress asked.

"Yes, I'll take the big daddy special with scrambled eggs," he said.

"And I'll take number one: eggs over easy," I added.

"What do you want to drink?"

"I'll take a small orange juice and some water," Charlie replied.

Our conversation became quiet.

"Well, continue with your story, Louis," Charlie requested.

"I've been in Omaha since Thursday. I drove my truck here to see my son, daughter-in-law, and my grandkids. A lot of my family traveled from around the country to see us. It was supposed to be sort of a family reunion Thanksgiving dinner. It was supposed to be a fun, relaxing, and peaceful get-together, but it turned out to be anything but that."

"Well, what happened to change all of that?"

"It's a long story, but I can tell the gist of it."

"I've got some time. I don't have to be anywhere until about 9:30," Charlie replied as he looked at his watch. "Well go on, continue."

"First, it started with me almost killing my nine-year-old granddaughter with my car, and then our Thanksgiving turned into a shouting match with our Aunt Hilda, my sister, who had to be rushed to the hospital emergency room for choking to death on food," I blurted it out so concisely.

Charlie's eyes opened wide not expecting to hear so much bad news so quickly.

"That's not all. There's a whole lot more."

"You can tell me."

"We waited in the ER at Methodist Hospital for over 14 hours to later find out the next day that my sister had died."

"I am so sorry. My prayers will be with you," Charlie said as he placed his hand on my shoulder to try to comfort me. I looked a little squeamish, as I felt uncomfortable with a stranger placing his hand on me.

"We were so exhausted from the ER wait at the hospital that we left for my son's house after we heard from my sister's doctor. We headed for my son's house hoping we could get some sleep after that traumatic event, but we found something awful waiting for us," my voice began to shake.

"When we pulled into the driveway, we found the front door standing wide open. Then we turned on the lights and found nothing but total destruction and devastation," I raised my voice with anger.

"What do you mean by total destruction and devastation? I mean, how bad could it have been?"

"Every piece of furniture and everything that is breakable was smashed and cut into pieces. Feces was smeared on the walls with ugly obscenities. There were knives stuck into the walls. Their cat was carved up into pieces and left for them to find in their pantry. The water was left running on the toilet and the bathtub upstairs. It flooded the entire house. And to make matters worse, my son and his wife were robbed of all of their money and valuables stored in a safe," I said bitterly as I was trying to calm down.

There was a long, still silence. Charlie looked me in the eyes compassionately and shook his head in disbelief.

"I'm sure you've got to wonder where God was when all of this happened," Charlie said sympathetically. "But God was there. He saw it all."

"But how could God have let this happen?"

The Contrary

"Everything happens for a reason. God didn't cause all of this to happen. God could have allowed this to happen for a reason yet to be known at some later time. Sounds like you and your family are going through some fierce battles and trials right now. But God never gives us more than we can handle. We all go through battles and trials in our lives. I don't want to seem like I don't care because I do. But when we go through these difficult times, it makes us so much stronger than before. It builds our character so we can face tougher times up ahead in our lives."

"You speak like you're an authority on this. Sounds like you know what you're talking about."

"Well, I've had some personal hardships in my life. My congregation has experienced many tragic calamities in their lives. You could say I know what I'm talking about," Charlie confidently replied.

"Are you telling me you're a preacher? You mean I've been talking to a man of God all of this time, and I didn't even know it?"

"Yes. I've been a pastor for over 25 years."

"What church do you work at and where?"

"I'm pastor at St. Mark's Lutheran Church down the street."

"What time is your service?"

"It isn't until 11:15. I don't need to be there until about 9:45 a.m. You act kind of surprised that I'm a pastor."

"Well, I haven't met too many pastors that are so easy to talk to like you. Usually they seem unreachable, kind of like trying to get in touch with God."

"Wow, that's an interesting connection between your perception of pastors and God. Hopefully we're all approachable. We represent God in our everyday business and work. God is here all the time watching and listening, even when it doesn't seem so. Sometimes maybe we're the ones who have distanced ourselves from God. You're invited to the service if you'd like to come. You're always welcome."

"No thanks. I'll pass today."

There was a lull in their conversation until Charlie broke it with a question.

"So do they have any suspects, any leads?"

"They caught him. But I'll get to that in a minute," I continued the story. "After we discovered the total destruction and walked through every corner of the house, we called the police. The detective arrived and searched the entire house. He made a report on it, my son called his homeowner's insurance company, and that's the last we thought we'd hear from them.

We ended up having to stay at the Holiday Inn because we had no place to go. Then they called us the next day and asked us to come down to the police station. We all hurried to the station and waited for them to call us to the interrogation room. There's where it ended up being an ugly heated battle of butting heads, if you'll excuse my French," I raised my voice. "To our complete surprise, we discovered that the suspect was one of our family members."

"He was a family member?" Charlie asked.

"Yes, to make everything even worse, the criminal happened to be my nephew Adrian," I said as my voice cracked with emotion.

"Oh, that's awful, Louis."

"What's awful is that he confessed to the crime earlier when he was caught doing the same crime to a neighbor's house. And what made matters even worse was that my son and daughter-in-law got into a heated argument with me over the whole thing."

"What for?"

"Well, the detective wanted them to press charges against Adrian since it was their house that had been robbed and ransacked. They hemmed and hawed around, sitting on the fence for the longest time. They couldn't decide whether or not to press charges since it was one of our family members. I had my opinion about it, too. That's what started it all," I said emphatically. "I told them to stop being such wishy-washy bleeding-heart liberals and throw the book at him."

"So what did you want them to do to Adrian?"

"My son and daughter-in-law kept talking about how we needed to forgive Adrian if we have love in our hearts. But I felt like they needed to throw him in jail or give him the chair. They were worried that it would ruin Adrian's life and that he would always have this around with him for life with a police record and all. I told them in no uncertain terms that if they let him go scot-free that he would just do the same thing over and over again. I know criminals, and they end up being repeat offenders."

"You didn't have any more faith in your nephew than that? I mean, did you ever think that there could be some hope for him or that God could change his life through prayer and counseling?"

"No, I don't believe that at all."

"Well, if God could send his son to Earth and forgive us for crucifying Him, why can't God forgive Adrian for what he has done?"

"I never thought of it that way," I replied. "But they ended up not pressing charges against him. I was so angry that I didn't want to speak to them for days. I'm sure they didn't want to speak to me either."

"Well it's a shame that it had to come down to that," Charlie replied trying to understand it all.

"Then that night I had this awful dream that seemed real. There was a woman's voice calling my name over and over again."

"Who was it?"

"There was this bright blinding pillar of light. A woman with large wings, golden hair, and fair complexion was speaking to me. She was floating over my bed for a very long time."

"Are you telling me there was an angel in your dreams?"

"Yes. She told me so," I explained. "After I refused to acknowledge her for the longest time, she became agitated with me and was so persistent that I couldn't help but listen to her. What made matters worse is that she told me that I was not dreaming and that she was real."

"What did she want?"

"She came to warn me that something bad was about to happen to me if I didn't change my heart and ways."

"You say that something bad is going to happen to you? You mean like a premonition?" Charlie asked curiously.

"Yes, perhaps. And this wasn't the first time that she appeared to me. She made herself known to me the night before in a surprise appearance that lasted for well over an hour," I confessed.

"It doesn't sound like a dream to me. And it doesn't sound like you're losing your mind either," Charlie replied trying to analyze it all. "It could well be an apparition."

"An apparition, what's that?"

"There are plenty of stories in the *Bible* of apparitions. You don't even have to be that holy to see one," Charlie joked with me. "I'm not saying that you're not holy. I'm saying that those who experienced apparitions in the *Bible* were not that holy."

"Should I be concerned about the angel's warning?"

"She could very well be warning you of some major event in your life to come. What did she say you needed to do to change your ways and heart?"

"This angel told me that I was cruel, mean-spirited, and didn't have any love in my heart," I replied seeming agitated that Charlie would ask me.

"Do you think that is true?"

"I just tell the truth."

"What is the truth?"

"The truth as I know it to be," I said emphatically.

"Well, there are a lot of things in our lifetime that we hear or learn about that we believe to be the truth, when really the truth is found in only one place, the *Bible*, God's word. You know things like 'Love thy neighbor as thyself.' 'Do onto others as you would have them do onto you.' Those are some basic truths for starters. There are a lot of people who believe what they want to believe. Some even go as far as to rewrite the whole *Bible*. The truth is a funny thing. Many people in this world believe what they say to be the literal truth."

"The angel told me that I was disrespectful and rude to my brothers and sisters because I thought that what I believed was the truth and the only truth. She said I was harshly judgmental and self-righteous because I didn't agree with everyone else in what they did or said."

"Wow, that's a mouthful."

"Yes and the angel said that I was an angry, bitter, and mean-spirited old man."

"Wow, that angel has a lot of nerve."

"You're telling me," I replied. "At first I ignored her. I blew it off as a bad dream or a nightmare. But then when she reappeared again for the second time, I began to do some thinking. She said that I needed to ask people whom I have mistreated to forgive me for treating them so cruelly."

"Did she hint at when you needed to make this bold change?"

"She was emphatic about me making those changes immediately. But how do you make changes like that so quickly?"

"Well, it starts with asking God to forgive you. But you must repent of your sins first," Charlie advised.

"I feel like I'm basically a good person," I confessed.

"No one's good, Louis, not even me. It says it right here in the *Bible* that no one is considered good. We have all fallen short of the glory of God, and we are all sinners," Charlie said confidently.

"Well, now I've heard it all. We are all a bunch of wicked no-good sinners," I said sarcastically.

"I didn't mean it that way, Louis. I just meant that God says in His word that we have all fallen short of His glory. We aren't perfect because we aren't God," Charlie tried to defend what he had said.

"The angel said that I didn't think before I spoke. She said that is why I don't have any friends and why I've pushed my family as far away from me as I have. I never realized that all those words I said could hurt or anger people."

"Oh, yes, words are very cutting and hurtful. They can be like sharp daggers stabbing us deeply. In fact, if we aren't careful with what we say, we can destroy someone with our words. We can leave lasting wounds that won't heal. That is what's so damaging in relationships. Do you think you have always been this way?"

"What way?"

"You know the angry, bitter, mean-spirited person the angel claimed that you are?"

"I'm not sure. Let me think. Norris, my son, says that I used to be kinder and more loving than I am now."

"Well, when was that?"

"He claims that in the days when I was with his mom, which was Samantha my wife, I was basically a nice guy. But he says that all changed in me after Samantha."

"What happened to Samantha?"

I choked up with tears. I held my head down low and started crying. Charlie reached over to place his arm around my shoulders to comfort me.

"I lost her to cancer. She was the best friend I ever had," I said through my tears. "We had been together happily for 45 years."

I continued to openly weep. I couldn't control myself. I felt all the sadness and pain of losing her come over me all at once like a giant bolt of thunder striking a tall old oak tree.

"The day before she left this Earth she somehow managed to write her last words to me in a letter. She was so weak but she somehow still found the strength to write those words. I hold onto her letter with my dear life."

There was again silence.

"I know that this must be very difficult on you. I am sorry for your loss," Charlie said sympathetically.

"That same thing happened to me about ten years ago before I remarried. I had been married to what I considered to be my soul mate. We were together since high school. We were ninth grade sweethearts. She was my best friend, too," Charlie continued as he started to well up with tears showing in his eyes.

"One day, unexpectedly, her life was taken by a drunk driver. She was killed in an awful car. I thought I would never get over that horribly tragic day. But somehow through the grace of God and through God's mercy I met a sweet, beautiful, and kind woman whom I now call my wife. I know you never really get over the hurt and the pain. But somehow God replaces that hurt and pain with his joy," Charlie confidently said.

"So you see there is hope for you, Louis, if you trust God. He can take all of your hurt, pain, bitterness, and anger that you are feeling and replace it with joy, love, kindness, and happiness. Just think about it, will you? And remember God loves you today as he has always loved you. He still loves you no matter what you've done to him or to others. He is a mighty merciful and forgiving God," Charlie reminded me.

Charlie stood from the stool and I stood after him. Charlie gave me the biggest warmest hug that anyone had given me in a long time. I felt genuinely loved. I could feel God's love, too, for the first time in a very long time.

"Let me get this for you, Louis," Charlie requested as he took my check and his to the cash register. Charlie paid for both meals and left a rather large tip on the counter.

Charlie and I left the Waffle House and headed toward our cars.

"It was great to meet you, Louis. Everything is going to turn out fine. Remember God is in control. I will remember you in prayer."

"Thank you, Pastor Charlie. I will think about what you said. I will always remember this day," I said with kindness and gratefulness.

Charlie got into his car and headed to his church to lead the 11:15 a.m. service.

I got into my truck. Before I started it to leave, I sat there for the longest time. I thought about all Pastor Charlie had said. I thought that what Charlie said could very well be true as to why I was bitter, mean-spirited, and judgmental. And I thought that if I truly were that cruel as a person how would I ever change my ways. I continued to think about it all—how I was going to change my attitude and my relationship with Norris and Julie.

I felt as if I was going to do any changing I should start soon. I wasn't sure how to go about it and when. I also thought about the angel's warnings. They sent shivers down my body thinking about what could happen to me if I didn't change soon. I became fearful and paranoid because I thought something bad could happen to me at any minute. I started my truck and headed cautiously back to my hotel. Everything was about to change. I just didn't know it yet.

CHAPTER SIXTEEN

TRYING TO MAKE AMENDS

I pulled my truck into the hotel parking lot and got out. I headed to the elevator in the main lobby and took it to the fifth floor. It was about 10 a.m. I thought that my son and daughter-in-law would probably be awake by now. I decided to pay them a visit. I stood in front of their door and knocked a few times. There was no answer. I knocked again a little louder. Still there was no answer.

This is strange that they're not answering their door.

I tried again with no success. I unlocked my room and decided to come back a little later to visit my son and daughter-in-law.

I sat quietly in my room by the desk. The solitary time gave me a chance to reflect on my life. I thought about how I used to feel when I had Samantha. My lovely and endearing wife made me feel alive. There was so much joy and love in my heart back then, not the emptiness I felt now. I realized how much I had depended on Samantha for my happiness. She was always around. We ate breakfast, lunch, and dinner together. We played together, laughed together, and cried together. I relied heavily on what Samantha thought. I worshipped her. I valued her opinions so much that all of my thoughts revolved around what Samantha believed. Those were happy days. I always wore a big smile. I treated people with respect and valued their opinions. When I had an opposite opinion, I usually kept it to myself.

How did I get so far off track in such a short time? How did I get to this place where I'm now, a hardened, bitter, angry, and mean-spirited man?

I slowly and carefully opened Samantha's letter that I held dear to my heart. I read her sweet and fragile words that she wrote to me the day before she went to be with Jesus. I wept silently. Oh how my heart ached with deep pain.

Then I thought about all the friends and family members that I had hurt along the way. I thought about what they thought about me. I felt ashamed for the way I had treated them.

Is it possible that I am still angry with God?

Am I still blaming God for Samantha's cancer?

Have I been taking my anger out on my friends and family all this time?

Scenes of past heated arguments with friends and family ran through my mind. They haunted me. Again I felt ashamed for how I had tongue-lashed all those people with my harsh, brutal words. I thought about what the angel had told me saying I had destroyed and wounded many lives because of my sharp divisive words that cut like knives. I realized that something was missing in my life. It wasn't just Samantha that was missing—it was peace, joy, love, and happiness. Oh, how I longed for those perfect elements of life. It made me shiver all over to think that I had lost them.

How could I get them back in my life? How could I once again fill that giant void in my heart? How could I win back the trust, love, and respect from the friends and family members

The Contrary

whom I had pushed away by being such a spiteful, despicable, and judgmental old man? I thought about it some more. I was lost for exactly what to do. I thought about what the angel advised me to do and how hard it would be to accomplish all of that. It seemed so overwhelming to me and yet, according to the angel, it was simple. I had to ask for forgiveness from those whom I had hurt. I had to throw away all of my pride, admit all of my mistakes, and basically start over. That meant repenting before God. I wasn't sure if I was ready to humble myself that much. That might mean that I would have to hold my tongue and keep my opinions to myself so that I could show unconditional love to people even if I didn't agree with them or like them. That was an awful lot to ask of me to change. I thought about how that would make me feel and look to others. I felt naked and vulnerable. Yet I realized I needed to quickly make some major changes in my life before something catastrophic would change it for me.

The clock on my hotel wall read 1:30 p.m. Had I been in deep thought for over three and half hours? I thought to myself how serious my problems were. My problems started to consume me like a burning fire. My problems were about to overtake my life. I thought that Norris and Julie might be at their hotel room by now. It was after lunch time on a Sunday afternoon and maybe they had settled back into their rooms and were spending some time with Michael and Sadie. I knew what I had to do. I had to pay my son and daughter-in-law a visit and ask them for forgiveness. I got out of my chair and left my room, closing the door behind me. I stood in front of Norris and Julie's room. I knocked loudly and firmly on the door. There was no answer. I knocked again. Finally, Norris came to the door.

"What do you want?" Norris asked grumpily.

"I've got something important and urgent to tell you," I replied with a contrite voice.

"Is it about that angel again?" Norris asked as he spoke to me through the gap in the door where the chained lock was hanging.

"No, it isn't about that."

"Haven't you hurt us enough, Dad?"

"You're right, Son, I have hurt you," I said apologetically.

"When did you come to realize that?"

"It's a long story. It has to do with the way I've felt before and after your mom," I revealed some of my feelings to Norris.

"Really?"

"Yes, really. Are you going to invite me in or just make me stand out here in the hallway talking to you through the crack in the door?"

"Julie is very hurt and angry with you. Right now she doesn't want to see you."

"Understood. But this is urgent, Son. If Julie doesn't want to see me right now, maybe we could go somewhere and talk."

"Okay, wait right there. I'll ask Julie."

I waited in the hallway. I could hear words between Norris and Julie in the background but couldn't quite understand what they were saying to each other. I continued to wait outside their door for about ten minutes. Finally Norris returned to the gap in the door.

"Okay, Dad, I'll meet you in the lobby in five minutes."

I breathed a sigh of relief that my son was willing to talk, even if my daughter-in-law didn't want to see me. I headed to the elevator and took it down to the lobby. I waited for Norris on the couch near the main desk.

It was still and quiet. It seemed like the longest time sitting there in the lobby. Suddenly the lobby elevator door opened and Norris stepped out.

"Okay, Dad, I'm here. Where do you want to go to talk?"

"Let's go somewhere where we can talk without being interrupted."

The Contrary

"You mean like a park? Somewhere where there are no people around so that in case we should erupt into violence, no one will see us? I've learned my lesson with you, Dad. I won't be suckered into a shouting and screaming match like in the past ever again. But we can go to the park down the street. We don't even need our cars, Dad. It's only three short blocks of walking."

"Okay, let's go to the park," I agreed as we exited the hotel. "It's a beautiful, pleasant day."

"It is rather warm for a November Nebraska day," Norris continued the small talk.

"Did you tell Julie where we were going?"

"No, I just told her that you and I were going to meet to talk. She knows how to find me if she needs me."

"Not many people out on a sunny day like this."

"I guess they think it's a cold Nebraska day like it usually is about this time of year," Norris replied as we turned the corner and reached the block where the park was located.

"Here we are. And there happens to be no one around, lucky us. Which bench do you want to sit on?"

"How about this one?" I pointed to the bench facing the statue and fountain located in the center of the park.

"Okay, fine. Now what is so important and urgent that you need to talk?"

"I want to talk to you about me and my unacceptable rude behavior."

"You don't have to tell me that, Dad. I already know about your behavior. Julie and I have had to put up with it for well over four years."

"Well, that's what I've come here to tell you. I'm sorry," I said as I held my head down low.

"Sorry for what—making our lives a living hell for the last four years?"

"I have been mean-spirited and judgmental to you and

Julie," I confessed.

"You could say that. That's putting it mildly. You've been a monster. Yes, you have. Ever since mom died, something's drastically changed with you, Dad."

I sat there and listened to my son vent his anger and frustration at me.

"You used to be a kind-hearted Christian. You used to love us for who we were, not for what we stood for. And suddenly after mom died, you jumped on this gigantic bandwagon and started preaching all of your right-wing radical nutty beliefs."

"Wait just a minute. Just because you don't believe the way that I do, doesn't mean you have the right to call them right-wing radical nutty beliefs. I resent that. I came here to apologize to you and Julie for all the years I have treated you wrong," I said with a sincere voice.

"Apologize? Is that because of your angelic dreams? Did your angel tell you to apologize or what?"

"I came to apologize to you from my heart."

"What's the ulterior motive, Dad? What have you got up your sleeve?"

"Absolutely nothing, Son."

"Yeah right, do you expect me to believe that? I'm not falling for that forgiveness crap," Norris said heatedly. "I mean, you suddenly decide to apologize after giving us four years of living hell. Do you expect me to believe it's for real? How am I supposed to believe your apology is for real?"

"I guess through trust and faith. That's all I have to go by—my word."

Norris shrugged his shoulders in disbelief. He had a hard time believing I was sincere.

"How do I know you won't start that crap again after apologizing to Julie and me?"

"Well, you don't. You just have to trust me."

"Trust you? I haven't trusted you in a very long time."

"That's sad. That hurts me. I'm still your dad, you know. I would love more than anything to see us love each other again and learn how to trust each other as fathers and sons do."

It was difficult for me to get those words out. It was even harder for me to admit my mistakes to my own son.

"How do you suppose that will happen?" Norris asked.

"By you forgiving me for the way I have treated you and Julie over the years. That's a start."

"Forgiveness is hypocrisy if you're going to start doing the same ugly things over again."

"Can't you see, Son, I am genuinely sincere about apologizing?"

"Sincere? I'm not feeling it, Dad. I still think there is an ulterior motive behind you asking me to forgive you."

"Well, I don't know how to make this any clearer than what I am doing now."

"You're going to have to give me some time to think this all through. You pull all of this mean crap on us for years and then run to me begging me to forgive you. This doesn't make any sense."

"Can't someone have an awakening? Can't someone see the error of their ways?"

Norris shook his head in disbelief.

"You, Dad, changing *your* ways? I don't think so. You're going to have to show me a whole lot more change than this before I'm going to think about forgiving you."

Those words from my son were sheer frustration for me. I had hoped that my son would show some mercy. I had hoped that my son would forgive me for all of the mean ways of my past.

Why were my words not convincing enough to my son? Why wasn't my son feeling my pain and remorse? What would it take to convince him I was truly sorry for the way I had treated him over the years? These were questions that I was agonizing over in my mind.

"Well, Dad, I think we've had all that we can say to each other today. I'm going to head back to the hotel and see what Julie and the kids are up to. Are you walking with me?"

"You go on, Son. I'm going to sit here for a while and think about what you said."

"You do that. I'll see you sometime later at the hotel," Norris said as he walked away from me.

I sat on the park bench and stared into space. I watched as my son walked until I couldn't see him anymore.

What was I going to do? How was I going to convince my son that I was truly sorry?

I agonized over those burning questions in my mind. I was stumped for what to do.

Hadn't I been sincere? Why was my son acting that way toward me, questioning my motives and not trusting me?

Perhaps my son had too much anger and pain inside his heart to accept my forgiveness. Perhaps my son needed more time to think it over. Maybe my son couldn't just accept my forgiveness. Maybe he had some personal issues to work through in his mind and heart. I hadn't anticipated how difficult it would be to ask my son to accept my forgiveness. It seemed like a simple and easy thing to do for someone to accept your apology. But his anger and pain seemed to run too deep for that to happen anytime soon. His anger and pain was like the root of an old oak tree that had taken hold of the ground and was not about to surrender.

It appeared to me that the act of my son forgiving me would take longer time than expected. The problem was that I didn't have a lot of time left. The clock was running out.

Would I have any more unexpected visits from the angel? Was the last time the very last time I would see her again?

I was fearful and paranoid. I was going to have to watch every step I took as if it were my last, for I didn't know what to

The Contrary

expect or when.

    I stood from the park bench and walked toward the hotel where I was staying. I was watchful, looking forward, backward, and over my shoulders as I walked. I felt sad. My heart hurt with anguish over the fact that my son wouldn't accept my forgiveness. I was scared about the consequence, too, for I could feel that time was running out.

CHAPTER SEVENTEEN

THE FINAL WARNING

I arrived at my hotel at 4:30 p.m. after meeting with my son. I had walked longer than I had expected. Strolling through the streets of Omaha gave me time to think about the perilous situation and how to resolve it. I took the lobby elevator to the fifth floor and headed to my hotel door. I unlocked it and decided to take a nice long nap. I was exhausted. Talking with my son and walking had drained me. My son's response was taxing. I was frustrated over my son's attitude toward me. I still couldn't believe that he would not accept my apology.

I stretched out on the bed. I made myself comfortable. I continued to rehash today's park scene where my son would not accept my apology. I played that scene over and over in my mind until I drifted off into a deep sleep.

I dreamed of pleasant things. I could see myself with my lovely wife Samantha, hand-in-hand running through a field of lilies. We were laughing and playing. I remembered all of those wonderful and joyous years I had spent with her. My dreams took me back to when my son was a child. I held Norris close and played games with him in his tree house in our backyard.

The Contrary

Times seemed simple back then. I cherished my son, and we both got along perfectly. I missed those days when there was perfect harmony. I yearned for those days to return.

All of a sudden my beautiful, almost-real dreams turned into a nightmare.

I heard a loud piercing woman's voice calling out my name.

"Louis, wake up at once."

I remembered that haunting familiar voice. It was the voice of the angel who appeared to me twice before. I reached for my glasses. The clock said it was only 7:30 p.m. It was dark outside, but my room was illuminated by a very bright blinding light.

"You're early this time." I shouted to the angelic figure hovering over my bed covered in the blinding light.

"Don't be funny, Louis. This is a serious matter. Your time has run out. Didn't I make myself clear the first time?"

"Yes, you did."

"And you did nothing about it?"

"I tried."

"You tried. What does that mean? Don't give me excuses," the angel said as she raised her voice.

"I'm not. I swear to you that I'm not," I replied with a trembling voice.

"Explain yourself."

"I tried to meet with my daughter-in-law to ask her for my forgiveness, but she refused to meet with me. The best I could do was to convince my son to have a meeting with me."

"How did that go?"

"We met at the park down the street. I told him sincerely that I wanted to apologize to him. He didn't take me seriously."

"That's because you did the whole thing backwards. You should have come to God first. Didn't you listen to anything I said?"

"Yes, I tried to," I replied with a timid, trembling voice.

"Don't you remember when I told you to take it to God? I told you that you first needed to get down on your knees and ask God to forgive you for your despicable behavior over the past four years."

"When was that? When did you tell me that?"

"Don't play dumb with me, Louis. I specifically sent the pastor friend to give you that message."

"You mean Charlie?"

"Yes, that's who I am talking about."

"But Charlie isn't an angel, is he?"

"No. You don't get it, do you? Louis, I spoke to you in a message through Reverend Charlie just like Jesus spoke to you through that old street man you completely wrote off yesterday when you went to visit the police station."

"Oh, that was you talking through Pastor Charlie."

"That was me. You just didn't recognize me."

"Well, was that a real man I was talking to or an angel?"

"Reverend Charlie is a real man with a real church. I had sent him through God to deliver to you a very important message."

"How was I supposed to know that was you?"

"Well, he is a Reverend, and he spent a lot of his time trying to help you. What more do you want? And what did you do after talking with him?"

"I thought a lot about it."

"You thought a lot about it but didn't do anything about it?"

"I tried to reach out to my son to apologize to him, but he wouldn't accept my apology," I replied defensively.

"Louis, Louis, think about it. It all starts with asking God to forgive you first and repenting of your sins."

"How is God going to help me?"

"If you believe that God is in control of your life, God can make it so much easier to apologize to the ones you have hurt if you first ask Him for forgiveness and repent."

The Contrary

"I never thought of it that way."

"If you don't start with asking God for forgiveness and repent, you could be hitting your head against the wall in frustration over and over again trying to get people to forgive you of your wrongdoings. God opens the way and makes asking for forgiveness much easier. But, unfortunately for you, the clock has run out. You must act now. Take heed to my last warning. There is disaster on the way. You must ask God for forgiveness and repent," the angel said emphatically.

"I'm afraid to."

"Afraid of what?"

"Afraid that I'm not good enough to come to God on my knees," I admitted to the angel.

"Good enough? I've got news for you, Louis, no one's good. If you're human, you're imperfect. You're a sinner who is destined to make mistakes. I'd be more afraid of what will happen to you if you don't get on your knees and ask for God's forgiveness. If I were you, I'd be trembling in my shoes right now."

The angel warned, "This is my final warning to you, Louis. It is up to you. God can't make you ask Him for forgiveness and repent. Only you can decide in your heart to do that. I will be praying for you." The angel's bright blinding light started to fade.

"I will be praying for you." The voice continued again as it faded and the angelic figure disappeared into the darkness. The clock read 8:30 p.m. I was wide awake. So many emotions raced through my heart and mind.

I knew that the angelic visit was real. I was afraid. I was lost for what to do. I was too proud to fall on my knees before God in forgiveness. I felt that was beneath me to do such a thing. I felt like I wasn't worthy of God. I felt like I had sinned too much and was a wicked person. How could God ever forgive me after all the despicable ways I had treated my family and friends?

Yet, at the same time, I was paralyzed with fear. Fear of what would happen to me in the days to come. What if I was struck by a car? What if I accidentally stepped out in front of a bus? What if I died in my sleep or died in a hotel fire? I started to let my imagination run away with me, thinking about all the dreadful things that could happen.

I let fear and frustration get the best of me. I bent over in my bed with my face buried between my knees. I wept uncontrollably. My mind was searching for the next move.

Should I go and knock on my son's door again and beg him for my forgiveness? Should I call all of my family and friends to ask them to forgive me?

I was running out of options. I couldn't bring myself to do what the angel insisted was the only thing to do—come before God on my knees. So I laid there on my bed in misery and decided to do nothing. I decided that the best plan would be to gradually work out forgiveness with my son, my daughter-in-law, and then friends and other family. I decided that it would all work out over time.

I decided against bringing my forgiveness directly to God. I would handle it in my own way and time. I figured it would gradually work itself out. I tried to reason with my heart and mind. Maybe the angel had spoken to me in a figurative manner. Maybe the angel meant that a disaster wouldn't strike me immediately but maybe over a longer time period. I convinced myself that it wasn't as urgent a matter as the angel had presented it to be. I convinced myself that everything would be all right.

I calmed myself down and decided to not bother my son or daughter-in-law. I had completely talked myself out of resolving the situation for now. I told myself that it wasn't urgent and that the good Lord would help me to resolve the problems I was facing. I felt exhausted again and mentally drained. I fell back onto the bed and stretched out. My eyes were growing heavy. I drifted into a deep sleep. I wasn't concerned about the consequences of doing nothing. The soft pillows and mattress felt good. That was all that mattered. I had convinced my heart and mind that it all could wait until tomorrow. But tomorrow couldn't have come too soon. I would soon experience a day like no other days in my life—a day I would never forget.

CHAPTER EIGHTEEN

THE DAY OF RECKONING

The bright Monday morning sunrise shone through the hotel window and woke me. The clock beside my bed read 7:30 a.m. I couldn't believe that I had slept for over 10 hours. I had such a stressful night that it had worn me out. I figured I needed the extra sleep to calm my frazzled nerves. I reached for my glasses on my nightstand and placed them carefully over my ears and nose. I looked cautiously around the room. There was no angel. The room was still and quiet for a Monday morning.

I took a moment to reflect on what had happened last night. This time I had been terrified by the angelic visit and yet I had calmed myself enough to fall into a deep sleep. I rolled out of bed, stretched my arms and legs, and took several long deep yawns. I took a shower, put on yesterday's clothes, and brushed my teeth.

I left my hotel room and headed toward the elevator. I decided not to disturb my son and daughter-in-law. They had planned on staying an extra week at the hotel while the clean-up crew worked on getting their house back in order. They had

The Contrary

arranged to take an extra week off from work because their house was in total disarray, and they planned on attending Hilda's funeral service on Wednesday. I took the elevator to the lobby and headed straight for the hotel breakfast bar. I fixed myself a helping of eggs, bacon, toast, and coffee. I found a table in the corner of the hotel restaurant. The place was not busy, as most hotel guests had checked out after the long Thanksgiving weekend. I sat there eating my breakfast and read the *Omaha World-Herald*.

Out of the corner of my eye, I caught a glimpse of some familiar faces. It was my son, daughter-in-law, and their kids. They were at the breakfast bar filling their plates with food. I kept on reading my paper, pretending not to notice them. I figured they wanted to be left alone and that they had enough of me for a while. Norris, Julie, Michael, and Sadie sat at a table on the opposite side of the room from me. I could see that they were spending some family time together, and I pretended to ignore them. Finally, after Norris had finished eating, he walked over to the table where I was sitting.

"Did you sleep well, Dad?"

"I was so exhausted from what happened last night that I ended up sleeping over 10 hours. So, yeah, you could say I slept well."

"What happened?" Norris asked as he read my body language. "Don't tell me another angel visit."

"Yes, and to tell you the truth, I was terrified."

Norris was curious of my use of the word *terrified*. He pulled up a chair and sat at my table.

"How were you terrified?"

"The angel visit was different this time."

"How was it different?"

"She was fed up with me because I hadn't done anything to change my mean-spirited despicable ways."

"You tried to reach out to me yesterday when we had our

meeting in the park. Doesn't that count for something?"

"Yes, but she emphatically stated that I must get on my knees and ask God to forgive me first."

"Do what? Get down on your knees, and ask God to forgive you?"

Norris laughed. He continued to laugh at what I had told him.

"Dad, that's the funniest thing you've told me in a long time that God wants you to get on your knees and repent of your sins. What else does God want you to do?" Norris asked as he continued to chuckle.

"I knew you wouldn't understand, Son. This isn't a laughing matter. I believe something bad is about to happen to me."

"Something bad is going to happen like what?"

"I could be in a terrible car accident or be hit by a bus or get caught in a hotel fire or…." I began as my son interrupted me.

"Let me stop you right now, Dad. Nothing bad is going to happen to you. God wouldn't do that to you."

"But the angel warned me that time was running out, and something disastrous was about to happen to me."

"First of all, Dad, those angelic visits were all dreams that seemed real. Second, God is a kind and loving God, he wouldn't do something awful to you. And last, I'm going to make sure nothing happens to you Dad because I still love you."

Norris stood and reached over to give me a warm and affectionate hug to comfort me. Norris believed that all of the stress from the Thanksgiving weekend had caused me to dream unpleasant and haunting dreams. After all, I had almost hit his daughter with my truck, had witnessed Hilda's traumatic death, and had visited their ransacked house earlier, not to mention all the stressful arguments we'd had during the weekend. All of those events would have made anyone have nightmares and hallucinations.

"It's going to be okay, Dad. I can reassure you that nothing bad is going to happen to you."

"Thank you, Son, for trying to make me feel better about all of this."

"You're welcome. I love you, Dad."

"I love you so much, Son."

I finished my breakfast and stood to give my son another hug. I was cautious about approaching Julie, Michael, and Sadie who were sitting at a table that seemed like a mile away. I still sensed cold, chilly feelings coming from them. I decided to leave them alone and to work out my forgiveness at a later time.

"Son, I'm going to the bank downtown to cash my Social Security check. I've been carrying this check around in my wallet for a good while. I need some cash since I'm running out of money."

"All right, Dad. I'll see you later."

I headed toward the front door and strolled to my truck whistling. As I started my truck, I thought of the warm embrace I had received from my son. It made me feel good inside. I felt like I had made some progress with my son, but was it enough to please the angel and God?

I continued to drive cautiously through the streets of downtown Omaha. I turned left, then right, and drove in different directions searching for a place to park on the street. Finally I found a parking space. I reached into my pocket and found some quarters to feed the meter. I strolled down the sidewalk toward the bank, a block away. I read the large sign above the elegant brass revolving doors: BANK OF OMAHA. The building was 14 stories tall and was covered in brick, which made it stand out over the other buildings, which were built with concrete.

I entered the revolving doors. I marveled at how large the bank was. I stopped and stared. I admired the gray marble floors and the high marble ceilings. The large brass chandelier hanging from the ceilings made the bank look more like an art museum. The teller windows were tall and made of pure gray marble. The sight of this museum-looking bank was a sight to see for a small town boy who was used to banks the size of trailers. There were only a few customers in the bank, so the lines were not long. Only three people stood ahead of me as I waited to cash my check. As I stood in line, I marveled at the large marble safe with a giant brass wheel that turned to lock it. There was an armed security guard standing close to the safe.

My mind wandered as I continued to wait in line. My mind flashed back to all of the calamities that had happened during this Thanksgiving weekend. I was in another world and wasn't paying attention when the teller called me to her counter.

"Next," the teller said as she raised her voice.

I was still daydreaming. A customer standing behind me had to tap me on the shoulder to wake me up.

"Sorry," I said.

I walked up to the teller and handed her my Social Security check.

"Good morning," she said to me.

"I'd like to cash this check."

"ID please."

"Oh, yes." I reached into my back pocket to retrieve my wallet. I found my driver's license and handed it to the teller.

The teller looked at it and then stared at me.

"Yes, that's you alright," she said with a smile.

The teller entered my check into the computer and the drawer opened. She handed me all of the bills.

"100, 200, 300, 400, 500, 600, 700, 800, 900, 1000, 1100, 1200, and 50 dollars."

She counted the money as she placed it in my hands.

"Here is your receipt."

I was happy that I now had money to spend while I was staying in Omaha. I soon forgot about my troubles. I had made up my mind that I was going to have a great day, angel or no

The Contrary

angel. I walked down the long, wide lobby with a smile on my face whistling a familiar tune.

Before I could reach the revolving door, a gang of five masked men stormed the building parading assault weapons and shouting at the top of their lungs.

"Everyone freeze. Get down on the floor and don't move!"

Everyone in the bank, including the tellers, fell to the floor with their hands placed behind their heads. The silence was overwhelming. The armed security guard standing in the corner pulled his automatic pistol and pointed it directly at the armed masked men. There was a stand-off: five men with assault weapons from Uzi's to AK-47's pointing their weapons at the one security guard who was pointing his automatic pistol back at them.

I had dropped to the floor. I was lying between the five men and the security guard. I was shaking all over. I was in a state of shock. Gruesome thoughts raced through my mind, and I desperately searched for answers for what to do.

"We ain't got time for this stinking piece of garbage. The cops will be here soon. Get rid of him," one of the masked men commanded.

There was a loud, rapid exchange of gunfire. Bullets ricocheted all over the place bouncing off the ceiling, floor, and walls of the bank. I dug myself deep into the marble floor with my face and body completely pressed against the floor.

Jesus, Lord God, help me. God help me. Don't let me die, I cried quietly to myself as bullets zipped by my head and body. I started shaking violently. I tried to control my tremors.

I swear, I promise to change my wicked ways if you'll save my life, I cried out quietly to God. The guns stopped firing and the bullets stopped flying. The armed security guard was slumped over in a pool of his own blood. Half of his brains were stuck to the vault walls. His eyes had been shot out and were missing. He had been shot over 200 times with the assault weapons. His body looked like shredded wheat. There was a woman lying on the floor who had been hit by stray bullets.

"Help me, someone help me," the woman moaned as if she held onto her last breath.

"Someone do something. Help her," a male customer pleaded to the armed masked men.

One of the men who appeared to be the leader strutted over to the injured woman pleading for mercy.

"I'll be glad to help you ma'am. I'll take you out of your misery," he laughed sadistically mocking her.

The masked man pointed his AK-47 directly at her face and open fired on her about 100 times which left her face unrecognizable. There was nothing but blood and shredded tissue.

"Do you feel better now?" he asked the lifeless corpse lying on the floor in front of him.

The male customer who had pleaded for the masked men to help the wounded woman screamed at the masked men.

"No! No! You cowards! How could do such a thing?"

The men started laughing uncontrollably at the male customer who was standing there helplessly.

Two of the men grabbed him by the shirt collar and dragged him out to the middle of the bank floor.

"Get down on your knees, close your eyes, and say your last prayer," the masked leader demanded.

"No, God, please, no," he cried out for mercy. "God, please spare me."

The sound of several assault weapons firing at the same time could be heard. The Uzi's and AK-47's were all aimed at the male customer crying and pleading for mercy.

There was silence. The male customer who was on his knees begging for mercy looked like a blob of blood and tissue with vital organs protruding. He was unrecognizable from being hit with over a 100 rounds of bullets. The masked men laughed sadistically.

"That will take care of him. He'll think next time before he opens his mouth."

I was lying on the floor frozen, pretending to be dead.

The masked men headed toward the opened bank vault with their large bags. They stuffed their bags with stacks of bills.

Sounds of multiple wailing sirens could be heard.

"Stupid pigs are here. They're here."

"Let's go."

The large brass revolving door started to move. The police were entering the building. The masked men dropped their bags stuffed with money and grabbed several tellers by the neck. I became squeamish because my bladder was filled. I couldn't hold it much longer. My body started to move on the floor. One of the men noticed that I wasn't dead and grabbed me by the back of my shirt dragging me over to the teller window area. One of the men grabbed a clump of my hair and held onto it with one hand. He shoved the barrel of the AK-47 deep into my ear.

"Lord Jesus, Mother Mary, ahhh," I screamed with intense pain as one masked man held my body up with a clump of my hair.

"God, please, God, please help me," I cried and shouted for mercy.

"God's not going to help you, you scumbag old man," the masked man shouted back with laughter.

By then, the police had entered the bank building and had drawn their .45 automatic pistols at the five masked men. Realizing that the masked men had assault weapons and they only had pistols, the police froze but continued to point their weapons at the men. The police looked around and saw that several people including myself were being held hostage.

"I wouldn't radio for backup if you know what's best for you," the masked leader shouted to the police standing about 30 feet from them. "Put your weapons down and lay down on the floor slowly."

The four police officers hesitated. But they knew they were outgunned and outnumbered so they laid their pistols on the marble floor. The four police officers sank to the floor with their faces pointing to the floor.

"They obey," the masked leader said laughing and mocking them.

"Those dirty bastards. They deserve to die. Get rid of them now," the masked leaded commanded with a loud and evil sounding voice.

Loud, long rounds of gunfire could be heard echoing through the bank walls. Hundreds of bullets struck the four officers lying on the floor. Their bodies violently jerked and twitched in reaction to being struck.

There was complete silence.

The masked leader walked over to the dead officers lying on the floor and kicked their bodies in protest.

"You worthless pigs," he shouted at their lifeless shredded bodies. "You had to go and screw up our plans," the masked leader ranted as he blamed the police for his foiled bank robbery. "Why couldn't this have been easy? We go in and get the money and leave without getting caught."

The police standing outside the bank heard the gunfire and realized that their fellow officers who had entered the building were in grave danger or had possibly been injured or killed. They called for more back-up.

The SWAT team arrived and surrounded the bank building. They shouted on megaphones to the masked men inside.

"We've got you surrounded. Come out with your hands on your heads."

The masked leader who was holding me by a clump of my hair with an AK-47 pointed deep into my ear put his arm violently around my neck. I gasped for breath, choking and coughing. The masked leader paraded me through the revolving door and stood pointing the barrel of the AK-47 inside my ear.

"Let us go with the money, and we won't hurt anyone," he shouted angrily at the SWAT team members and police.

"We've got three hostages, and we will kill them like we did your cop buddies."

The SWAT team realizing that they had a crisis on their hands backed away from the building. They decided to let the masked leader seize the moment for the time being. The SWAT team commander and his team huddled around each other to devise a plan on how to capture the masked men without getting any more innocent people killed. The police weren't sure how many bank robbers they were dealing with.

The bank was surrounded by television cameras and reporters. The network shows that were already in progress in Omaha were interrupted and television viewers were watching the hostage-drama bank robbery live from their television screens.

The standoff between the five masked men holding three hostages and the police with reinforcements from the SWAT team continued.

The masked leader dragged me by the locks of my hair through the revolving door and pulled my body next to one of the teller windows. I was screaming and wailing at the top of my lungs with intense agony and pain. The other masked men held three tellers at gunpoint.

"We're going to break out of this bank one way or another," the masked leader shouted angrily.

Time continued to pass with the standoff. Meanwhile outside the bank, the local media and television shows were continuing to broadcast live. CNN and Fox News had arrived and were covering the hostage situation live.

"We're coming to you live from downtown Omaha,

Nebraska, where a four-hour standoff between five dangerously armed masked men and the Omaha Police continues. The SWAT team has completely surrounded the downtown Bank of Omaha. As many as seven, possibly eight, hostages are being held at gunpoint," the CNN reporter said as she stood in front of the camera on the street facing the bank.

"The masked men holding the hostages are believed to be carrying deadly assault weapons such as Uzi, AK-47, and M16 rifles. You are watching CNN, the most trusted network."

At the same time, a Fox News reporter stood about 15 feet from the CNN reporter on the same side of the street.

"Fox News has just learned that five masked men stormed into the Bank of Omaha in Nebraska earlier today. Four police officers and one bank security guard are believed to be dead. There are at least seven people being held hostage. One hostage is identified as Louis Green of Griswold, Iowa. The 68-year-old man was seen earlier being held at gunpoint by a masked man standing in front of the downtown Bank of Omaha," the Fox News reporter said. "You are watching Fox News, fair and balanced."

Back at the hotel, Norris had kicked back and was relaxing with Julie and the kids. Julie was soaking in the Jacuzzi in the hotel bathroom. Michael and Sadie were playing video games. Norris was channel surfing when he saw the breaking news on CNN.

"Julie, come quick."

"What is it?"

"It's about Dad."

Julie grabbed a huge bath towel to cover her body and ran into the adjoining room to watch the story on the large flat screen television.

"Oh my God, something's happened to Louis," Julie shouted as tears started to show on her face.

"68-year-old Louis Green was seen earlier today outside of

The Contrary

the downtown Bank of Omaha being held hostage at gunpoint by a masked man."

"That's Dad they're talking about. We've got to do something," Norris shouted with anger. "Come on everyone, we're getting out of here. We're going to the bank," Norris ordered his family to hurry out of the hotel room, so they could get downtown as fast as possible.

Julie dried herself off and threw on some clothes. They hurried to the elevator. When they reached the lobby, they sprinted out of the front door and jumped into their car. They sped away to the downtown area. When they arrived in downtown Omaha, they found the streets barricaded and a large crowd of spectators, gawkers, and news reporters.

Norris, Julie, and the kids parked their car several blocks away and sprinted toward the Bank of Omaha. They pushed and shoved their way through the crowd. As they reached the front of the crowd there was a yellow-roped area marked POLICE LINE: DO NOT CROSS. Norris and Julie forced their way through the front of the line but were stopped by the police.

"Sir, ma'am, no one is allowed past this point," the officer shouted.

"But that's my dad in there being held hostage."

"Sir, you can't go past this point."

Norris was heated and emotional. He continued to force his way past the restricted area. Several police officers grabbed his arms and shoulders and forcefully led him away from the yellow-roped police line.

The CNN reporter overheard Norris shouting something about his dad being held as a hostage and insisted on an interview.

"This is CNN live coming to you from downtown Omaha, Nebraska," the reporter said as she held a microphone pointed at Norris.

"We are talking with Norris Green of Omaha, Nebraska. I understand that your father Louis Green is one of the hostages being held by the five masked men in the bank."

"Yes, Louis Green is my dad," Norris replied as he tried to hold back the tears that had overcome his face.

"We understand that he is still alive. We know that you must be feeling a great deal of anxiety and pain not knowing if your father will make it out alive. There are already four police officers confirmed dead and one bank security guard who was killed because of those deadly assault weapons. How do you feel about this tragic story?" The CNN reported asked.

"I am saddened by this tragic news. My heart goes out to the family and loved ones of the people killed today. People shouldn't be allowed to own or use these dangerous and deadly assault weapons. I strongly urge Congress and the President to pass stricter gun control laws prohibiting the use of these guns."

"Thank you Mr. Green for your interview. We wish you and your dad the very best. We hope that your father will be released alive and unharmed."

Norris, Julie, and the kids stood on the street staring at that bank looking scared and helpless.

"If ever Dad needed an angel, it would be now. He could use an angel right now," Norris said to Julie with a discouraged voice.

Back at the bank, the masked leader with the help of his four accomplices neatly lined up the four hostages including me against the marbled bank wall. The masked leader had released his hand from my clump of hair. I was halfway standing up leaning against the wall. I was feeling weak from the emotional trauma and stress that I had endured. I hadn't had anything to eat or drink since 7:30 a.m. It was now 1:30 p.m. I was in a great deal of pain from having my hair nearly torn out from my scalp.

"Okay, which one of you wants to die first?" the masked leader asked as he pointed his AK-47 rifle at the hostages lined up against the wall.

"Someone's going to die every three minutes unless one of your worthless, scumbag, dumb-asses finds a way for us to get out of here alive."

The other hostages were frozen in a state of shock and had terror written all over their faces. They were weak from the emotional trauma and from not eating or drinking anything. Earlier they had witnessed the brutal murder of the bank security guard, four police officers, and two bank customers. They were emotionally exhausted.

"Let's start with you," the masked leader said as he pointed his AK-47 rifle at the center of my forehead.

"Speak now or you die. What is the plan for getting out of here?"

Before I could answer or the masked leader could pull the trigger, a bright blinding pillar of light shone down at the center of the bank building. A towering, broad-shouldered woman with large feathered wings appeared.

The sight of the angelic figure standing there covered in the bright, blinding light startled the masked men.

"I wouldn't do that if I were you," the angel warned the masked leader with his finger on the trigger of his AK-47 pointed at me.

"Who's going to stop me, bitch?" the masked leader shouted angrily back at the angel.

"I don't think you know who you're talking to. And I'm not a bitch, thank you."

Hearing those words coming directly from the angelic figure, the masked men started laughing uncontrollably.

"She isn't real. We're seeing things. We've been in here way too long. Take this, bitch," the masked leader shouted at the angelic figure as he fired many rounds of ammunition at her.

The other masked men followed by firing rounds from their guns at the angelic figure.

"You can't kill me no matter how hard you try," she said to them after they stopped firing.

The masked men looked puzzled in disbelief. Their eyes had nearly popped out of their sockets seeing how the angel was still standing alive and well.

"Boys, boys, don't say I didn't warn you."

Suddenly the AK-47's, M16's and Uzi rifles slipped out of their hands and rose to the ceiling. The weapons were suspended and were floating high above them.

The masked leader realizing that he and his partners were without weapons reached from behind and pulled out a sharp eight-inch hunting knife. He made a lunge at me trying to kill me.

Suddenly the knife the leader was holding slipped out of his hands and was floating above him with the assault weapons next to the ceiling.

The masked men were perplexed and dumbfounded about how their guns and knife ended up floating above their heads. They shouted angry obscenities at the angel. They shook their fists.

"You have made Heaven very sad today because of your despicable actions against your brothers and sisters and because you stole from this bank. You killed seven people all because of greed," the angel lectured them.

"No one tells us what to do, bitch," the masked leader shouted back at the angel.

"Yeah, you judgmental, self-righteous bitch," the other men shouted and spat on the floor in defiance.

The assault weapons floating high above them began firing multiple rounds of ammunition. The weapons were positioned in such a way that they fired close to the masked men and their leader without actually striking them. There were bullets flying everywhere. It was a spectacle to see: five masked men jerking, jumping, dancing, screaming, and begging for mercy. The scene looked like five masked men tap dancing to hip-hop. The guns continued firing for several minutes.

"Stop, stop, stop," the masked men screamed and begged for mercy from the angel.

When the bullets finally stopped flying, there was silence.

"You need to apologize to Louis and the people in this bank for terrorizing their lives," the angel demanded with a loud authoritative voice.

"Never, never, no chance in hell," the men shouted at the angel.

The assault weapons fired rapidly again all around the five masked men. The guns were positioned so that the bullets firing would not strike any of the masked men, just make them dance and feel the pressure of intimidation.

"Stop, stop, stop," the masked leader shouted and begged for mercy again.

There was silence again as the guns stopped firing.

"Are you ready to give up and apologize?"

"Never," they shouted back as if their voices started to grow hoarse from crying and shouting.

Then not just one miracle happened, but seven miracles all at once. The bank security guard who was slumped over dead in a pool of his own blood suddenly woke up and became alive. His shredded, bullet-ridden body was instantly healed including his face where his eyes had been shot out. He looked as good as he did before the masked men shot him. The bank security guard picked up his pistol lying on the floor next to him and stood. Witnessing this miraculous occurrence of a body suddenly being resurrected in front of their eyes caused the masked men to scream and huddle together with fear.

"What the hell?" The men were trembling with fear as the resurrected bank security guard aimed his pistol at them.

"Freeze. Put your hands over your head and don't move," the resurrected security guard demanded.

The four dead police officers who were lying in a pool of blood on the floor were also resurrected. The bullet wounds all over their bodies became instantly healed. The resurrected officers grabbed their guns lying on the floor next to them and stood up. The resurrected police officers aimed their guns at the masked men.

"Freeze."

"Don't move. We've got you surrounded," the masked men were scared beyond belief. They were violently trembling with fear. Underneath their masks their faces had terror written all over them.

"Don't shoot," the masked leader pleaded. "I beg you don't shoot."

The masked men stood helplessly with their hands over their heads in surrender.

The two bank customers who had been brutally executed by the masked leader resurrected. They opened their eyes and stood. There was not a single wound on either of their bodies.

The masked men screamed and begged for mercy. Never in their lives had they seen seven bodies resurrect from the dead. They were terrified.

Suddenly one of the assault rifles fell from the ceiling and landed perfectly in my hands.

"This is for you Louis," the angel said. "You are a hero today. You are going to march these sick humans out of the bank with their hands above their heads, and you're going to force them out with your gun."

"Say you're sorry to all of these people you have robbed and killed," the angel demanded of the masked men.

There was complete silence from the masked men.

"I can't hear you," the angel demanded again. "Say you're sorry."

Again there was silence. The masked men refused to talk.

"Okay, Louis, it is time for us to get this show on the road.

Line them up in single file," the angel demanded.

I pointed my gun at the masked men and ordered them to line up in single file. The masked men did as I commanded. They stood in single file with their hands raised and placed on their heads in surrender.

"Okay, Louis, you're going to march them out of this bank in front of all of those people. The police can take it from there. Remember you are a hero, Louis," the angel said as the bright pillar of light started to fade. "You are a hero, Louis."

The masked men lined up in a single file and walked through the bank and through the large revolving door. I led the resurrected police officers and security guard as they followed behind with loaded guns.

The police and SWAT team aimed their weapons at the masked men as they paraded out of the bank with their hands held above their heads. The masked men were completely surrounded by the police. I paraded out of the bank with my assault weapon still pointed at the masked men. The resurrected police officers, the resurrected bank customers, and all of the hostages followed. The crowd of spectators and gawkers suddenly went wild. There was a long roar of applause and cheering similar to the noise after a Super Bowl win.

The police officers apprehended the masked men and handcuffed them. The officers removed each mask so that their identities could be revealed. The crowd wildly booed them as they watched each mask come off. It was a very humiliating experience for the masked men. It was as if they were in an ancient Roman arena where they were getting ready to be fed to the lions.

Realizing that I was the hero, reporters rushed over to interview me.

"How does it feel to be alive?" the CNN reporter asked.

"It feels amazing to be alive," I replied breathing a sigh of relief as emotional tears filled my face.

"How did you capture these dangerous armed masked men?" the Fox News reporter asked.

"It's a long story," I replied as I tried to hold back my tears.

"Do you care to elaborate?" the Fox News reporter asked.

"Not at this time. I'm exhausted," I replied as I tried to catch my breath.

Reporter after reporter surrounded me. The scene looked like a presidential press conference. I was completely exhausted and emotionally worn. Norris, Julie, Michael, and Sadie pushed and shoved their way through the crowd and ran up to hug and kiss me.

"Dad, you're alive," Norris shouted with joy as he held me in his arms.

"Thank God you're alive," Julie shouted as tears streamed down her cheeks.

Michael and Sadie wrapped their arms around me.

"Granddaddy, you're okay."

"I'm so lucky and blessed to be standing here with you this very minute," I cried out to them.

"Let's get you out of this zoo and back to our hotel so you can get some rest," Norris said to me.

"I'm exhausted and starving, too," I appeared to be in a state of shock.

Before I could leave, the police approached me with a few questions.

"We need some answers from you on this hostage-bank robbery tragedy that occurred today."

"I am totally exhausted and famished. Could I get some rest and food first?"

"Sure. Let me get some information from you as to where to find you."

I gave the officer all of my contact information.

"Thank you, sir. Here is my card. You can call me at the police station when you are feeling better. We are so glad that

The Contrary

you are alive," the officer said to me as he let me go.

Norris and Julie helped me to their car realizing that I was in no shape to drive.

They helped me with getting into the car since I was disoriented and in a state of shock.

Norris, Julie, Michael, Sadie, and I all headed back to our hotel to get some food and rest.

All of our past arguments, conflicts, and differences were instantly forgotten. Now all they could think about was how thankful they were that I was alive. Mean-spirited, cantankerous, and despicable didn't matter at this point. It seemed as if I had become a changed man. But they would have to wait until tomorrow to see how much I had changed after my state of shock wore off. Tomorrow would be another day. Hopefully it would be a far better day than today.

CHAPTER NINETEEN

WHAT A DIFFERENCE A DAY MAKES

I was so exhausted that both Norris and Julie with the help of the kids had to carry me from their car into the hotel lobby. My arms were draped around Norris and Julie's shoulders as they helped me into the elevator that took us to the fifth floor. I didn't say a word as they carried me to my hotel room. I was drained of every ounce of energy. Norris unlocked my hotel door. They carried me in and carefully placed me in a comfortable position on my bed.

"Dad, are you okay?"

I could barely nod my head but did so to show my son I was all right.

"Look, if you absolutely need anything, please call me. I will be there for you, Dad," Norris said with a tender loving voice.

I nodded my head again. Norris, Julie, and the kids reached over to give me hugs and kisses. They left my room and headed to their room to get a good night's sleep. They also were exhausted.

I was too exhausted to brush my teeth or change my clothes. I fell into a deep sleep and left all of the troubles of this world

The Contrary

behind me.

Tuesday morning greeted me with a bright light of the sun piercing through my window. I reached over to my night stand to find my glasses. I placed them carefully over my nose and ears. The clock in my room read 10:03 a.m. I had slept nearly 14 hours. I was in a complete daze and had trouble waking up. I continued yawning uncontrollably. I reached for my cell phone beside my bed. The cell phone was flashing as if it was giving some kind of warning. I checked it and discovered that I had over 40 voicemail messages. Suddenly, the hotel phone rang next to my bed. I answered it.

"Is this Louis Green?"

"Yes," I said with a groggy, hoarse voice.

"This is the hotel front desk. We have been calling your room all morning, but no one answered."

"What do you want?" I asked hesitantly.

"There are people asking for you. The whole hotel parking lot is full of reporters looking for you, sir. What do I tell them?"

"Wait just a minute."

I placed the phone down by my bed and walked over to my window. I peeked out of the corner of the drapes to see what the clerk was talking about.

I was flabbergasted and amazed. There were what looked like a crowd of at least 100 people gathered around the hotel with cameras and large microphones. The trucks in the parking lot were from CNN, FOX, CBS, NBC, ABC, PBS, and NPR. The local news stations were represented too. There were satellite dishes raised above the trucks. It looked as though the reporters were camped out for some major news event. I walked back to my bed and picked up the phone.

"I see what you mean. Holy crap, do all of these people want to talk to me?"

"Yes, I'm afraid so."

"Well, thanks for the warning. Tell them I'll be down

shortly."

I felt much better than yesterday. My adrenaline was kicking in and flowing strong. I felt energetic again. I washed up in the shower, brushed my teeth, combed my hair, and put on my clothes.

I locked my hotel door behind me and walked toward the elevator. I decided not to disturb my son and daughter-in-law since they were probably still sleeping.

I took the elevator down to the hotel lobby. As I stepped out of the front door of the hotel, there was loud thunderous applause and cheering from the crowd.

"Louis. Louis. Louis, you're our hero," the crowd continually shouted with praise.

I was bombarded by questions from reporters. Microphones and cameras were being shoved into my face. There were voices coming from all directions. I stared out into the crowd with a glazed look. I didn't say a word for the longest time.

"Speech, speech, speech," the crowd loudly clapped and chanted together.

Finally, I gained my composure and came back to reality.

"Do you realize that you are a national hero today?" The CNN reporter asked me as she tried to get a comment. The CNN report was live breaking news to the nation with a caption that read: LOUIS GREEN HAILED AS HERO IN THE BANK OF OMAHA ROBBERY/HOSTAGE TAKEOVER.

"Well, I hadn't given it much thought," I answered as the crowd started laughing at my humility.

"You are definitely a hero, Mr. Green," the CNN reporter replied. "How did you manage to capture those masked men?"

I thought about the question for a minute. *If I tell her an angel had helped me, she will laugh and think I'm crazy.* I knew that she wouldn't believe me, so I told her what she wanted to hear.

"It was luck. I had a lucky break."

Another reporter from CBS news pushed her way over

The Contrary

toward me.

"We had a report that the four police officers had been killed in the bank. How did they make it out alive?" The woman reporter at CBS News asked.

I thought about it for minute before I answered.

If I tell them that the four police officers had truly died but were resurrected by an angel, I will be the laughing stock of the world.

"They were always alive. The report of the police officers being killed was erroneous."

"We interviewed the police officers who were reportedly killed, and they don't remember anything. It's if they are suffering from amnesia or something similar," the CBS News reporter said to me.

"It was a false report. They were always alive," I insisted.

"So you're saying that the police officers helped you capture the masked men, but they don't remember doing so?" the CBS reporter grilled me.

"It was something like that."

An NBC reporter managed to reach me.

"It appears that no one was killed in the hostage takeover of the Bank of Omaha yesterday. How is that possible when there are confirmed reports of four police officers killed and others possibly killed?" the male NBC reporter asked me.

"It looks like those confirmed reports were not accurate. There was no one killed in the Bank of Omaha yesterday," I told the NBC reporter as I was trying to cover for the *hard-to-explain miracles* with an angel that occurred yesterday. They would never believe me in a million years, so it was best that I not mention the angel and resurrection stories period.

A Fox News reporter inched his way toward me and finally was able to ask me a few questions.

"There are a lot of strange things that happened yesterday at the hostage takeover that can't be explained. Would you care to explain?" the woman reporter of Fox News asked me.

"It was a robbery and a hostage takeover. Through luck, we were able to break free and capture the robbers," I explained as I raised my voice in jubilation.

"But you were up against all odds—five masked men armed with assault weapons. Supposedly the four police officers, the security guard, and some customers were killed. How is that possible that you could have overcome such odds?" The woman reporter at Fox News asked.

"First of all, no one was killed. I repeat no one was killed. And luck was on our side as we caught them off guard," I replied as I tried to explain to them how it really happened.

About the time more news reporters started swarming in on me, my son arrived. Norris pushed his way through the crowd trying to reach me. He surrounded me, trying to protect me from the crowd of reporters. Then the news reporters started asking Norris questions.

"We understand that you are the son of Louis Green. What do you know about the bank robbery and hostage takeover of yesterday?" an ABC news reporter asked Norris.

"No comment, no comment." Norris answered like a lawyer would at a press conference when he didn't want to answer the question.

"How do you think your dad managed to capture those dangerously armed masked men in the bank without being killed or harmed?" an NPR news reporter asked Norris.

"No comment, no comment."

"What are you doing, Son? You're not answering their questions," I whispered in my son's ear.

"It's none of their business. What went on in that bank yesterday should remain private until the trial is held," Norris replied to me whispering in my ear. "You could say something that could be used against you in a court of law."

I realized my son was right about not answering all of those questions from the news reporters. I could say something incriminating or something that might persuade the jury to change their minds when the bank robbery-hostage takeover case came to trial. Still it was thrilling being recognized by all of those reporters and being lavished by all of their attention. I turned to the crowd of reporters and spoke what was on my mind.

"I am done answering questions. Thank you," I emphatically shouted over top of all the clamor of the crowd. "Thank you for your loving support and encouragement. But I must go now," I turned to walk away from the crowd.

The reporters ignored my request to end the questions. They continued to follow me as Norris helped me to the front hotel door.

"Sir, sir, what do you have to say about...."

"How did you escape from...."

There was an uproar and barrage of questions being rapidly fired at me from the reporters pushing and shoving to follow Norris and me into the hotel. Norris rushed us to the back stairwell instead of waiting on the elevator, so we could avoid the reporters. Norris helped me up the five flights of stairs until we reached the hotel rooms. Norris and I unlocked my hotel room, and we sat on the bed trying to catch our breath.

"Wow, I think we ditched them," Norris said.

"They were like a swarm of bees coming down on us, Son."

Norris grabbed the remote to the flat screen television and turned it to the news channels.

"You're all over the news on every channel, Dad. It seems like they can't get enough of you. Next thing you know, you'll become a household word," Norris said to me laughingly.

"Ahh, finally we've got some peace and quiet. No crowds, no noise. Just the way I like it. When I woke up this morning I had 40 voicemail messages waiting for me on my phone," I said.

"Why don't you check them now? It could be about Hilda's funeral for tomorrow."

"Sure, why not."

I checked my voicemail messages as Norris kicked back and relaxed catching up on the news on television. Time passed as the clock in my hotel room read 11:55 a.m.

Finally I had finished checking all of my messages.

"So what were all those messages about?"

"It's unreal, totally unreal."

"What's unreal?"

"You won't believe who just called."

"Who called?" Norris asked.

"They want me to be a guest on the *After Hours Show*."

"No way," Norris said.

"Yes way. And the people from the *Prime Time Show* want me to make an appearance too."

"Get out of here."

"And *Good Morning America*, *CBS This Morning*, *The Today Show*, *Fox and Friends*, *All Things Considered*, *The Ellen Show*, and *The View* all called asking me to be their guests," I said proudly.

"Wow, that's quite a line-up. What are you going to do? You'll be spending your whole life making appearances on those shows."

"I guess I'll do as many as I possibly can," I shouted excitedly.

"I don't know if I would rush into any of those quite yet," Norris advised.

"They are just like reporters. They might pry something out of you that you didn't mean to say. Next thing you know, your words are being used against you in court to persuade a jury how to make their decisions. I'd think long and hard before I said anything that I might regret later."

"Changing the subject, Son, we need to talk."

"Okay, Dad, what do you want to talk about? You have my undivided attention," Norris looked me straight in the eyes.

"I know you might not have believed me the other day in

the park when I asked you to forgive me for my despicable ways, but I am ready to change, ready to be a new man," I confessed.

There was a long pause of silence. Norris thought about what I said.

"Okay, Dad, so what do you want me to do?"

"I am begging you to please forgive me for all of the ugly ways I have treated you over the years. Please forgive me for the cruel and despicable things I have said to you, too," I cried begging for mercy.

There was more silence. Norris continued to think about what I had just asked of him. He thought about all I had been through in the last 24 hours. He imagined how stressful and painful my life had been being subjected to the Bank of Omaha robbery and how I had been held hostage yesterday. Norris was grateful that I was alive and unharmed.

Norris's eyes welled up with a flood of tears. He ran over to me and gave me a long, warm embrace.

"Yes, Dad, I forgive you. I love you so much, Dad."

I reacted by returning a warm embrace. I was overcome with a flood of tears. My face showed deep emotional feelings of affection for my son.

I breathed a deep sigh of relief.

"Do you know how long I've been waiting to tell you this? I've wanted to ask you to forgive me for a long time," I said with deep affection.

"Yes, and it feels good to get all this off of our chests," Norris breathed a deep sigh of relief.

Norris and I told each other some jokes, cutting up, laughing, and playing as dads and sons sometimes do to break up a serious moment.

"I sure hope Julie, Michael, and Sadie can forgive me."

"I believe they will come around. They have seen your heart change for good. I think they admire your hero qualities too."

"I'm thankful for that."

"Why don't you get some rest, Dad, and we'll meet up for lunch around 1:30 p.m."

"Okay, Son, will do. Love you," I said as my son left my room and closed the door behind him.

I stretched out on my bed and propped a soft pillow under my head. I reveled in the fact that my son had just forgiven me. To me that was a milestone achieved. I felt a quiet, peaceful feeling come over me. I was overcome with joy. The act of my son forgiving me made up for all of the terror and pain that I faced during that bank robbery and hostage takeover crisis yesterday. I smiled and fell asleep. The last words I told myself were that Julie, Michael, and Sadie would finally come around and forgive me.

CHAPTER TWENTY

FORGIVENESS

I was snoring so loudly that I woke myself up from a long deep sleep. I reached over to my nightstand to find my glasses. I placed them carefully over my ears and nose. I was shocked that the clock read almost 4 p.m. I couldn't believe that I had missed lunch with my son and daughter-in-law. I picked up my cell phone and called my son.

"Norris, I fell asleep and just now got up. I was going to join you and Julie for lunch. I'm so sorry."

"That's perfectly okay, Dad. I know you must be exhausted from all that you've been through. I understand."

"Do you think I could meet with Julie, Michael, and Sadie for a little while down in the lobby? I have something important to tell them. I promise I'll be nice."

"Let me ask Julie, and I will call you right back."

"Okay, Son, I'll be here in my room waiting."

I stood and stretched my arms and legs. I took a few long deep breaths and yawned continuously.

My phone rang.

"Dad, it's me. Julie said she would get together with you in the hotel restaurant. She said Michael and Sadie would be joining you, too."

"That's perfect."

"She said to meet them at 5 p.m."

"Great. Tell Julie I will see her then."

"Okay, Dad, I'll let her know. Have a good meeting."

I hung up the phone. I was excited about Julie's willingness to meet with me. At the same time, I was nervous because I wasn't exactly sure how Julie would react to what I was about to tell her. I paced the floor of my hotel room looking at my watch nearly 20 times. It was only 40 minutes until I would meet with my daughter-in-law and grandchildren. The anticipation of telling Julie what was on my heart and mind was more than I could bear. I stood from my chair and walked nervously to the bathroom and back almost 200 times. I felt sick to my stomach. It was if I had developed a bad case of stage fright. Finally my watch read 4:55 p.m. I closed the hotel room door behind me and walked the fifth floor hall to the elevator. I took the elevator to the lobby. I walked toward the hotel restaurant and caught a glimpse of my daughter-in-law and grandchildren.

"I'm glad you were willing to get together with me," I said as Julie, Michael, Sadie took a seat next to me at a booth near the far end of the restaurant.

"It's good that we can finally talk," Julie replied nervously.

"Yes, it is indeed. This has got to be one of the hardest things I've ever done. But I need to get this off my chest."

Before I could say another word, a pretty waitress came over to our booth.

"Can I get you something to drink?"

"I'll have some coffee with no sugar or cream," Julie told the waitress.

"I'll have the same thing, too," I said.

The Contrary

"The kids will have bottled water, please," Julie added.

"Okay, I'll get those to you right away."

"So continue with what you were saying," Julie requested.

"I have been a jerk toward you and the kids for the past four years."

"That's saying it mildly don't you think?"

"Yeah, you're telling me. I'm so despicable that I can't stand myself," I said as I laughed jokingly. "Seriously though I have said many unkind, cruel, and mean words to you Julie, and I know that I have hurt your feelings."

"You have Louis, and it's been really painful. I have a lot of resentment built up against you. And the way you've treated Michael and Sadie over the years is uncalled for. I'm sure they resent it too. The trouble is that you speak what's on your mind without thinking first. You don't think about whether it will offend or hurt someone else. And you just blurt it out. You are, of course, entitled to your opinions. But you don't have to force your opinions on everyone else. I see how you and Norris butt heads. You are quite alike as father and son. You are both strong-headed and opinionated. But I wish that someday you two could get along and love each other more like a father and son are supposed to."

"I hear what you are saying, Julie. And I don't deny it. Everything you're saying is true. That is why I asked you to meet with me today."

"I'm so sorry to interrupt you all. Here are your drinks. Here are the menus. I'll come back in little while and take your orders," the waitress interjected.

"Thanks. This is fine for now. We'll let you know later if we need anything else," Julie said as she handed the menus back to the waitress.

"Everything that has happened to me lately has given me a change of heart. I have thought about it deeply. I realize the error of my ways. I realize that I need to change into a different person, a more likeable person," I confessed.

"Wow. That's a new side of you I haven't seen before. I must admit I like what I've seen of you lately. That took a lot of courage and bravery to overcome those armed masked men in that bank. And you were so humble after it all."

"Thanks. That's mighty kind of you to say," I continued, "My dear grandchildren, I haven't treated you kindly over the past few years. I've said some mean things and have treated you rudely. I am sorry for the way I treated you."

"That's okay, Grandpa. I forgive you," Michael ran to me and gave me a big hug.

"I'm sorry Sadie for yelling at you and telling you that you were stupid when I found you lying in the middle of the road last Thursday. I should have been more loving and caring."

Sadie smiled at me with approving eyes.

"That is sweet of you to apologize. I have been troubled by the whole thing since Thanksgiving Day. I can't believe I almost got killed and by my own grandpa," Sadie reflected.

"You've got to know I would never harm or hurt you."

"Yes, I know that Grandpa. It was an accident. But it was a mighty foolish thing for me to do. I realize now that no rosary beads are going to save me. You were right, Mom, Father Stewart never actually told me to go test God and lie down in the middle of the road. It's just that when Father Stewart told of the power of the rosary beads and how we could pray *Hail Mary's* to release that power, I guess I believed the rosary beads could actually stop cars from running over me. I believed that God wouldn't allow one of his own children to be harmed in any way. But now I know that it is still up to me not to act foolishly. I've been doing a lot of thinking about this. I'm learning that God does protect me, but I still have to act wisely."

"Wow. That's a whole lot of wisdom pouring out of the

mouth of such a young lady," I replied. "Anyway, I want to apologize to you Sadie for how I've treated you over the past few years. Please forgive me."

Sadie rushed over to me and gave me a gigantic hug. My face beamed from eye to eye with a big bright smile. It felt like 1,000 pounds had been lifted from my back and shoulders. Michael and Julie were smiling like it was a celebration of a lifetime.

"Julie, I owe you a huge apology. I have treated you like dirt. That's no way to treat a family member that you love, particularly your own daughter-in-law."

"You're right, Louis. My life has been living hell with you around. I know that's awful for me to say, but it's true. I've taken so many things you've done and said personally. You have hurt me deeply. You've angered me to a point where I never wanted to speak to you again. But you know what they say if you don't forgive someone and you carry it around with you, it can eat you up like cancer. I need to let it go and give up all of the hurt, anger, and pain."

I remained silent and listened to Julie unload all of her emotions on me.

"It was mighty big of you to meet with us and to offer your apologies. And I confess I might not be quite ready to accept your apology, but my heart tells me that it is the right thing to do. It's not healthy for me to keep carrying around all of these dark emotions. So I've decided to forgive you Louis for what you've done to me. I forgive you."

I stood from the table and rushed over to embrace Julie. I felt tons of boulders being lifted from my back and shoulders. Julie felt so light from releasing all of her pain, anger, and hurt that she felt like she was dancing on the clouds high in the sky. It was a joyous moment to see. There was unity and harmony restored in a deeply divided family. God and the angels in heaven must have been smiling and singing with joy. My life was suddenly changed before my very eyes. And to put it lightly, it was the beginning of a significant change in my life for the best. Julie, Norris, Michael, Sadie and I could all sleep peacefully tonight all because of forgiveness.

CHAPTER TWENTY-ONE

NO ORDINARY FUNERAL

Julie woke next to Norris in their hotel room. She looked at the clock on the wall which read 9:55 a.m. Thoughts raced through her mind about her meeting with me yesterday. Norris and the kids were still asleep. She kept thinking about the words that were said between us. It made her feel wonderful inside. She thought how amazing the act of forgiveness was, how people could go through their entire lives holding bitterness, anger, and hurt inside and suddenly it could all be lifted from them in an instance by the act of forgiveness. Julie thought about how well her relationship with me as my daughter-in-law could turn out to be in the future. For the brand-new-me seemed like a kind, loving, and gentle man. There were a lot of qualities that Julie admired about the new me. Suddenly it occurred to her that today was Wednesday, and Wednesday was the day when Aunt Hilda's funeral service was being held in Omaha. All the calamities and catastrophes over the period of six days had caused her to lose track of time and what day it was.

"Wake up, wake up, Norris," Julie said as she gently shook him.

"What? What time is it?" Norris asked groggily.

"Aunt Hilda's funeral service is today at 2 p.m. It's already 10:30."

"You're right, sweetheart. I almost forgot."

"Michael, Sadie, wake up," Norris said in a loud voice.

Michael and Sadie woke and looked around acting disoriented.

"Dad, Mom, what time is it?" Sadie asked.

"I want to go back to sleep," Michael protested.

"We need to get up and get ready for Aunt Hilda's funeral service," Norris replied.

Norris got out of bed and went straight for the bathroom. Julie helped Michael and Sadie wake up. Norris took a shower, dried himself, and put on yesterday's clothes.

"I'm finished. The bathroom is all yours," Norris said to Julie and the kids.

"Honey, we need to go shopping. We need to get some dress clothes for Aunt Hilda's funeral."

"We don't have a whole lot of time, but you're right. We've been wearing the same clothes for the past six days."

"You all get ready quickly. I'll check on Dad to see if he is up. When I get back, we can grab some lunch in the drive-thru, and buy some new clothes."

"Okay, we'll hurry as quickly as we can," Julie told Norris as she reached over to kiss him.

Julie, Michael, and Sadie rushed to take a shower and get dressed. Norris shut the hotel door behind him and walked over to my room. He knocked on the door loudly. There was no answer. He knocked again even louder than before.

"Who is it?"

"It's me."

"Me who?"

"Don't play games with me, Dad. You know who this is."

I opened my hotel room door and smiled at my son.

"I was just checking to make sure it wasn't one of those reporters trying to snoop around into my business."

Norris laughed at the suggestion that I thought he was a reporter.

"Come in."

"Are you ready?"

"Ready for what?"

"Don't you remember? Today is Aunt Hilda's funeral service. It's at 2 p.m. at the First Church of God here in Omaha."

"Yes, I do remember now. I almost forgot."

"It's easy to do. Look at all of the crazy things that have happened to us in the past five days."

"You're telling me."

"I think this must be a world record. I don't know any other families who have had so many things go wrong in such a short time."

"You're right. What happened to this family? How did we run into so much bad luck?"

"I really don't know. Uncle Hershel must be having a tough time right now. Today is when he has to finally say goodbye to his wife of 40 years. He has to lay her in the ground and go on with his life as if nothing ever happened."

"You're right. It is a sad day for Hershel."

"Speaking of the funeral service, Julie and the kids are getting ready right now, Dad. We're planning to make a run through the drive-thru at McDonalds. Then we are planning to stop at Kohl's to buy some dress clothes. We'd love for you to join us if you'd like."

"I'd love to join you."

"Let's meet downstairs in the lobby at 11:30 a.m."

"Okay, Son, I'll see you then."

Norris hugged me and closed the hotel door behind him. As Norris unlocked his hotel room door and settled in to wait for Julie and the kids to finish getting ready, I showered, shaved, and got dressed.

11:30 a.m. came quickly. I joined Norris, Julie and the kids in the downstairs lobby of the hotel.

"Is everyone ready?" Norris asked.

"Yes," Sadie replied.

"Dad, why don't you ride with us?" Norris asked me.

"I would love to."

We followed each other out to the parking lot and got into the car that Julie had brought to the hotel. It was an SUV and was roomier than Norris's gas saving Intelligent Car. We pulled out of the hotel parking lot and headed east on Main Street. There was a McDonalds on the right side about three blocks ahead.

"Let's stop there," Norris requested.

"Okay. Here we are," Julie said as she turned right and pulled up to the order menu.

"What does everyone want?"

"I'll take a Happy Meal," Michael said.

"I'll have a chicken wrap with bottled water," Sadie said.

"Dad, what do you want?" Norris asked.

"I'll have a number one with cheese, fries, and iced tea."

Julie and Norris both ordered salads with bottled water.

"That will be $36.12 with tax," the voice said.

Julie pulled around to the cashier and paid her. Then Julie drove to the pick-up window.

"Grandpa, here's your number one," Julie said as she shuffled bags and drinks in the car.

"Thank you."

"This is mine," Michael said as he grabbed the Happy Meal out of his mom's hands.

Julie handed Norris his salad and bottled water. She reached over to the back seat to give Sadie her chicken wrap.

Everyone was quiet while they ate. The only noise that could be heard was the unwrapping of paper, the sipping of straws,

The Contrary

and the munching of food being devoured.

Julie continued to drive. She turned east on Main Street. It seemed like she had been driving for over 15 minutes.

"Kohl's is on the right in this shopping center," Julie said as she pulled the car up to the parking lot.

Just about the time she parked, everyone but her had finished eating.

"It's now 12 noon. We need to make this quick. The church service starts at 2 p.m. and is about 25 minutes away. Let's meet back here at the car at 1 p.m. sharp," Julie said to Norris and me. "I'll take Michael and Sadie with me. You and Louis go pick out some clothes."

"Okay. We'll be back here at one," Norris replied.

Everyone got out of the car. Julie grabbed Michael and Sadie's hands and sprinted into Kohl's Department Store. Norris and I followed them.

Once we were in the store, Julie took Michael and Sadie to the children's section to help them pick out a suit and dress. Norris and I shopped in the men's section for suits, shirts, and ties. After Julie had helped Michael and Sadie choose what they wanted to wear, she ushered them over to the women's section to pick out an attractive dress to wear. Julie found a professional two-piece business dress colored in gray and black. After Julie tried it on, she hurried to the checkout aisle with Michael and Sadie. She paid for the clothes and rushed out the door to the parking lot as it was almost 1 p.m. Norris and I were standing outside in the parking lot beside the car.

"Did you find anything you liked?" Norris asked Julie and the kids.

"Yes. There were some nice things in there. We found what we were looking for. How about you, Norris and Grandpa? Did you find what you were looking for?"

"Yes, we did."

We got into the car and held the bags in our laps and put

some on the floor. We knew that we would have to make a quick change so we could be ready.

"Do you know the way to the church?" Norris asked Julie.

"Yes, I have the address and the GPS should take us to the place. We should be there at about 1:30 p.m."

"Let's look for a place to change that's close to the church."

There was a long period of silence on the drive to the church. It could have been from being tired, bored, or just having nothing to say to each other at the moment.

"We are getting close to the church," Julie said. "Look, there's a Philo's Super Gas store over there. We can all change and hopefully be at the church before 1:45 p.m. since it's only a few minutes away."

Julie parked the car, and we grabbed the bags to get dressed. Ten minutes passed, and we managed to get dressed in our funeral attire and meet back at the car.

"That's teamwork. We did it. We're all here and can now head to the church," Julie said proudly.

As we were driving to the parking lot, Norris noticed something wrong with my suit.

"What's this?" Norris asked as he examined some tags hanging from the back of my suit.

"You've got the price tags still hanging out on the back of your coat, Dad."

"Oops, I guess I forgot to remove them. Someone at the funeral will think I shoplifted this."

Norris yanked the tags off of the jacket.

"Everyone, check your clothes to make sure all the tags have been removed," Norris directed.

"We're here," Julie said as she pulled into the church parking lot.

"There are a lot of cars here," Norris observed.

"You're telling me. Hilda and Hershel have a lot of friends," I said. "Before we go inside, everyone check your clothes, your

The Contrary

hair, your teeth...."

"Funny, Dad. You're so funny."

Julie, Norris, the kids and I got out of the car and sprinted toward the church building. Since it was a nice 45-degree sunny day, there was a crowd gathered outside the front door. There were faces we had never seen before. Perhaps they were friends or co-workers of Hilda or Hershel. When we entered the church building, we were greeted by familiar faces.

"Hi Louis, hi Norris and Julie," a voice from the crowd shouted.

"Oh, hi Shirley and Joe," I replied as I recognized some of my cousins from Atlanta.

"We haven't seen you in ages," Norris said.

"It's so sad about what happened to Hilda," Julie added.

"You're telling me. She was a lovely person. I know that Hershel must be taking it hard," Shirley replied.

"She's in a better place now," Joe said as he tried to reassure them.

"Yes, she is," Julie agreed.

"Well, Louis, you're famous now. We've been watching you on every news channel," Joe said.

"Aw, it's nothing. They're making more out of it than they should."

"Louis, you're just plain too humble. That was a heroic thing you did saving all of those people and capturing those armed men in that bank."

"Well, if you say so."

Out of nowhere Hershel appeared. He tried to force a smile, but his hurt was so deep from losing his wife that his smile came out more like a sad frown. Still he warmly embraced Norris, Julie, Michael, Sadie and me.

"We are so sorry for your loss," Julie said trying to console him.

"I know it must be very hard for you right now," Norris

said.

"It has been. But the good Lord has given me strength and has comforted me through all of this," Hershel replied.

"If you need anything Hershel, we are here for you," Julie offered compassionately.

"Thank you, Julie. Well, the service is about to start, so I'm going to get ready."

We walked into the sanctuary and took a seat on the third row, which was reserved for family members.

A pretty golden-haired woman sang the prelude of the service. Her voice was sweet, pure, and angelic. Every seat in the sanctuary was completely filled. There were people standing in the back. The church was crowded beyond capacity. The church seated about 350 people but over 500 people were there to pay their final respects.

Hilda's casket was positioned at the front of the church near the altar. It was a beautiful mahogany casket with brass fittings around the ornate wood. Apparently, Hershel had decided that the service would be a closed casket service, so no one would view Hilda as she lay in her coffin.

After the singer finished her songs, the organ and piano played a beautiful duet together. Then there was complete silence. You couldn't even hear a breath or a whisper. Hershel, who was known as Pastor Hershel by his church members, stepped forward to the microphone by the lectern. He cleared his throat and began to speak.

"It is overwhelming to me to see such a large crowd here today of friends, co-workers, and family members paying their respects to Hilda. She is standing in Heaven today looking down at us and smiling.

"Hilda was a great friend, loving wife, and companion. She served the Lord well. We were about to celebrate our fortieth anniversary this Saturday when the Lord called her to Heaven." Hershel's voice broke with deep emotion.

The Contrary

"Jesus is standing right beside her right now," he could no longer hold back his tears and began to sob uncontrollably.

There was a long pause of silence. Everyone remained quiet waiting for Hershel to regain his composure.

Finally Pastor Hershel pulled himself together and spoke again.

"Jesus is standing beside Hilda and he is saying, 'Well done, my faithful servant'."

There was not a dry eye in the sanctuary. You could hear people sobbing and trying to hold back their tears from the front pews all the way to the back of the church. Pastor Hershel continued his tribute to Hilda, and after he finished, there was another beautiful song performed by the singer. The sweetness of her angelic voice soothed the hurt and tears of all of those who were mourning. When she had finished singing, Pastor Hershel stood by the lectern and spoke into the microphone.

"We have a lot of family members and close friends who knew Hilda. Would anyone like to step forward and say a few words in memory of Hilda?"

There was silence as everyone looked around to see who would be the first one to stand and give tribute to Hilda.

A petite woman who looked to be in her early 50's approached the microphone.

"I worked with Hilda at Sweet Crest Middle School for over 20 years. Hilda loved the kids. They loved her. There wasn't anything that she wouldn't do to help people in need. There was a time when she helped me. I was going through an ugly divorce, and I was left with four children to take care of as a single mother. My youngest child Jacie got sick and was in the hospital for a long time. We had so many hospital bills that we couldn't afford to pay them," The woman said as she lowered her head and her voice broke from crying.

"Hilda found out about our troubles and came to our rescue. She personally gave us money, but she also started a fund raising campaign at school to help raise money for us to pay our hospital bills," she continued with a wavering emotional voice.

"That was a mighty kind act of love on her part. I will...." the woman said as she was interrupted by a flood of tears.

"I will never forget it. Hilda, if you are listening, I thank you from the bottom of my heart. I love you," the woman cried out and as she reached her arms up to Heaven.

You could hear people sobbing and crying all around the church. Some people were wailing with tears.

The petite woman finished her eulogy and returned to her seat.

An attractive young woman who appeared to be about 18 years of age stood and walked to the lectern. She reached to lower the microphone and spoke.

"Some of you don't know me, but about six years ago I attended Sweet Crest Middle School. My name is Lauren. Mrs. Hilda was my teacher. She was a very good teacher. She was a mentor, a friend, and a mother to me when I lost my mother to cancer just before I turned 13 years old," the young woman began as her voice wavered with deep emotion.

"Mrs. Hilda and Pastor Hershel took me in for five years. They helped raise me in my teen years. They were both loving parents to me during that time. My father left us about a year before my mother went to Heaven. I still lovingly call Mrs. Hilda and Pastor Hershel my parents." Tears flooded Lauren's face.

"I will miss you dearly, Mrs. Hilda. I will never forget what you did for me, *Mom*," she said as her voice choked from the tears she could no longer contain.

Lauren finished her moving tribute and took her seat. The silence was snuffed out by the haunting sounds of all of the sniffling, sobbing, and crying that echoed through the church walls. I decided to rise from the pew and walk to the lectern to speak into the microphone.

"I'm Louis Green, brother of Hilda. Some of you know who I am."

Everyone became quiet as I started crying and trying to hold back my tears

"I have a confession to make to you all today," I said as I almost lost my composure from the tears flowing from my eyes.

"For the last four years I have been a ruthless, despicable, mean, and cruel man. I have treated my friends and family with contempt, forcing my opinions on them. I have been self-righteous, vindictive, and judgmental. And that's why I've lost most of my friends and family," I said as I held my head down in shame.

"What hurts the most is how I treated my own sister."

I tried to get my words to come out but was overcome by tears.

"I am ashamed of the cruel words I said to Hilda. I only wish that I could take them back. I was always dogging Hilda about her weight. I was always putting her down and making her feel worthless. Of course Hilda was a strong woman, and she could definitely stand up for herself. She wouldn't let me get away with talking to her like I did.

"But I know she must have taken all of my despicable words and actions to heart. It always hurts more when it comes from a family member, especially your own brother. I used to ridicule her for all the diet pills and diet plans that she subscribed to. I thought she was *foolish* and *gullible* to believe that all of those things really worked. Instead, I should have been more loving and supportive of her. I know it is difficult to lose weight, and she must have lived a life of frustration always trying to lose weight. I feel partly responsible for her death. Just last week on Thanksgiving Day, we were all gathered around the table as one big family. Hilda was sharing with us her amazing results from taking a new diet pill she had heard about on *The Dr. U Show*. I immediately started discrediting the diet pill and Dr. U. I ridiculed and humiliated her in front of the whole family saying how *gullible* she was for following all of those diet plans. She became provoked and agitated with me. Hilda ate as fast as she could and kept eating more and more food. That is when she started choking. A piece of food had gotten caught in her throat. We tried giving her CPR before the paramedics arrived. But when she arrived at the hospital, she went into a coma and never woke up."

It was quiet in the sanctuary. Everyone was shocked that I would say the things I did particularly at her funeral service. Family and friends were surprised to hear all of that coming out of my mouth.

I continued, "My sister was an amazing person. She was such a great teacher. Hilda was loving and kind. She had a generous heart and would help anyone in need. She was a loving and faithful wife to Hershel. I know that God must be smiling with her in Heaven and saying 'Job well done'. Hilda, if you're listening to me right now, I am truly sorry for all the mean and cruel things that I said to you. I am sorry for treating you so badly," I spoke sincerely from my heart.

There were gasps of surprise from startled family and friends sitting in the pews.

"People do change. I only wish you could see me now. I have decided to give up my ugly, despicable ways and replace them with unconditional love for others. If you were here right now, I would wrap my arms around you and tell you that I love you."

There was silence.

"Hilda, I love you so much. Please forgive me," I said as I broke down with uncontrollable sobbing. I stood there at the lectern with my head held down low in shame.

You could hear people sniffling, crying, and wailing as they reacted to my stark and honest confessions.

I sat quietly as Hershel rose to the microphone and asked,

"Anyone else want to pay tribute to Hilda?"

There was a pause of silence in the sanctuary.

Suddenly an important-looking, well-dressed woman about middle-age rose from her seat and walked to the microphone on the lectern.

"I'm Alicia Fairbanks, principal at Sweet Crest Middle School here in Omaha. Hilda taught under me for 23 years. There are no words to describe how amazing and wonderful she was," Ms. Fairbanks confessed as her voice filled with emotion.

"She was honored with *Teacher of the Year* for three years in a row in our school district. She was well-loved and well-respected by everyone," Ms. Fairbanks proudly boasted.

"Hilda was a dear friend to me for all of these years. I will always remember and cherish our friendship. I will miss her so much," she was overcome with emotion as her voice waivered.

It was quiet throughout the church. Then Ms. Fairbanks regained composure and strength in her voice.

"Hilda, we love you. Thank you for your long, excellent service and commitment," her voice rose with praise as she finished her tribute. Pastor Hershel took the microphone again.

He asked, "Anyone else?"

There were more than 10 additional tributes including students, faculty, family members, and friends. It was indeed a special moment. Hilda would have beamed from cheek to cheek from all the praise and dear words she had received.

After all the tributes from admirers of Hilda, Pastor Hershel said the Lord's Prayer. There was a closing song from the guest singer, and then the pallbearers walked slowly to the casket to lift and carry it to the long black hearse waiting to take Hilda's body to the cemetery.

Everyone stood to pay respect to Hilda as the pallbearers walked slowly out of the church carrying the casket. The casket was lifted and placed into the hearse. Silence took over as they closed the door. Everyone walked solemnly out of the church and got into their cars. The police motorcycle escorts lined up in front of the long black hearse as the cars formed the funeral processional behind it. The police escorts led the hearse and the funeral party of cars onto the street. The funeral party proceeded down Main Street with the police escorts and hearse leading. To any innocent bystander, it would have appeared to be a long line of several hundred cars following behind the hearse all with their lights on lined up in single file.

It was a sight to see as the funeral party continued down Main Street and headed toward the cemetery, which was located on the outskirts of Omaha. The funeral processional continued driving for about fifteen minutes until it arrived at the cemetery gates. The hearse continued to drive through the gates and around a windy gravel road until it reached the plot where she would be buried. As the pallbearers opened the hearse door and lifted Hilda's casket out, the funeral attendees, family, and friends parked their cars all along the side of the gravel road. They gathered around a tent and took seats next to the six-foot empty grave. As the casket was hoisted above the grave to be lowered, Pastor Hershel opened the graveside service with a few words.

"Family and friends, we are gathered here today to lay Hilda's body to its final resting place," Pastor Hershel said as he tried to hold back a flood of tears. His face was red from having cried all day.

Norris, Julie, Michael, Sadie and I were seated on the front row near the casket. We couldn't keep from wiping the tears off our faces. Flashbacks of joyous times with Hilda in her younger days ran through our minds. We remembered how happy Hilda and Hershel were together.

Last week's Thanksgiving Day dinner with Hilda lying on the floor choking to death still haunted me. That traumatic ordeal in the hospital emergency room with Hilda fighting for

The Contrary

her life and then losing it was bone-chilling.

Pastor Hershel continued to give tribute to Hilda and then closed with a prayer. Pastor Hershel turned toward the casket. He bent down, placed a long-stemmed rose on the casket and kissed the casket with his final goodbye to Hilda. Pastor Hershel's face was covered in tears and he was shaking. I helped him back to his seat. I placed my arm around Hershel to comfort him. Then the casket was lowered into the ground until it reached the bottom. Everyone remained seated through the moment of silence. Family and friends gave each other consoling embraces and kisses as they headed back to their cars to leave.

"Hershel, I'm sorry for your loss of Hilda. She was a dear sister and lovely person. She will be missed," I said with my deepest sincerity.

"I will be leaving tomorrow for Griswold. I will be thinking about you and praying for you. Call or come visit me anytime, Hershel," I wrapped my arms around my brother-in-law.

"We love you, Hershel. We feel the pain you are going through. Call or stop by anytime," Julie sympathized as she embraced him.

"Goodbye, Uncle Hershel. You are an inspiration to me. Aunt Hilda will be missed. I love you," Norris said as he embraced his uncle.

As I walked with Norris, Julie, Michael, and Sadie back to their car to leave the cemetery, something strange caught my eye. As I turned around to see it more clearly, I caught a glimpse of what appeared to be an angelic figure standing several feet away from Hilda's grave. I thought it was a monument designed in the shape of an angel. But the angelic figure was moving and had wings. I took a good look at it. The flashback of my angelic visits at the hotel seemed all too real.

Am I seeing things? Is this really an angel? Could this be the same angel who visited me those times in my hotel room?

Before I turned around to catch up with Norris, Julie, Michael, and Sadie, I thought I saw the angelic figure smiling at me. Chills ran through my body and the hair on my arms stood up.

I turned around and continued to walk forward at a fast pace until I reached the car. As I got in the car and closed the door, Norris began to drive off. I took one last peek out the back window. The angelic figure was still there and continued to smile at me.

Could this be real? Could this be a sign of what's to come?

We all headed back to our hotel to get a good night's rest. It had been a long stressful and emotionally draining day for the Green family. I was leaving tomorrow for Griswold, and Norris, Julie, and the kids would be heading back to their ransacked house to start their long road ahead of restoring their home. The Green family returned to their hotel and made the trek to the elevator and down the fifth floor once again. Norris, Julie, and kids told me goodnight and then headed straight to bed feeling exhausted.

As I lay in my bed, I thought about the angelic woman figure that I saw in the cemetery smiling at me. I would be driving back to Griswold tomorrow, but I couldn't stop feeling a new sense of worry.

Could there be more danger up ahead? Is something bad going to happen to me?

Despite the unanswered questions, I fell fast asleep.

CHAPTER TWENTY-TWO

A HERO'S HOMETOWN WELCOME

"Yes he's on his way," the voice said confidently on the other end of the phone.

"He left about ten minutes ago and should be there around noon, so look out for him," the voice continued.

"Good luck with everything," the voice said as he hung up the phone.

I headed out in my truck to make the hour journey home from Omaha to Griswold. I had already had breakfast with Norris, Julie, and the kids. And they had already said their goodbyes with hugs and kisses.

As I merged onto U.S. highway 29 and headed east toward my hometown, my mind drifted. My mind flashed back to Thanksgiving Day when I arrived in Omaha and fast-forwarded to yesterday when I was paying my final respects to my sister Hilda. When I thought about all of the calamities and tragedies that I had been through in the last week, it gave me cold shivers. I thought about how lucky I was to be alive from that violent and humiliating bank robbery-hostage incident. I could never remember a string of continuous tragedies and calamities ever happening to me in my lifetime. I reflected on how my life had changed and how I was a completely different man then I was before the bank robbery-hostage tragedy. I remembered vividly those angelic visits I had experienced back at the hotel in Omaha. They seemed so life-like to me. And then the angel appearance in the bank seemed so real. It haunted me to think about how those bodies of the police officers, innocent victims, and the security guard had all resurrected before my eyes. I couldn't understand how that could be possible. I remembered reading in the *Bible* that bodies would be resurrected in the end times in *Revelation* when Jesus would return. But I didn't ever remember reading about bodies resurrecting in the present times. I thought it was best not to tell anyone—news reporters, friends or family about those bodies being resurrected by an angel. They would surely think I was insane and would recommend that I be committed to an institution.

I continued to drive on highway 29. I was about 20 minutes away from my hometown Griswold. I had only been gone for a week, but I missed my town and the people there. I loved the simple life in a town where everyone knew me by name.

As I kept driving, I could not seem to forget that painful memory of my sister lying there on the floor fighting for her life on Thanksgiving Day. Guilt continued to haunt my memory. I wasn't exactly sure how I was going to put that memory to rest.

Sure I had asked Hilda to forgive me at her funeral. But it was still not the same as speaking to her face to face and asking her to forgive me. I wished that Hilda was still alive, so I could tell her in person. Time continued to pass until the clock on the truck dashboard read 11:52 a.m. The excitement of returning to my hometown caused my heartbeat to race. I couldn't believe that I was only a few miles outside of town.

"There he is," the officer spoke into his two-way radio from his motorcycle waiting on the side the road.

"He should be arriving about noon. So be ready," the officer

The Contrary

continued as he warned his fellow officers on his radio.

Before I could reach the Griswold town limits, I could see blue lights flashing from behind me in my rearview mirror. I heard loud sirens and noticed several officers on motorcycles motioning for me to pull over. The sirens startled me. Afraid that I was in trouble with the law, I pulled my truck over to the side of the road.

The officers on the motorcycles pulled off to the side of the road behind me. The officers got off of their motorcycles and walked over to my truck. I rolled down the window to greet the officers.

"Louis Green, how are you?" one of the officers asked donning a big friendly smile.

"Is there a problem Bill, I mean, Officer Jones?" I asked.

"No, absolutely not, we are here to welcome you home. We are going to escort you into town. We have a big surprise for you," one of the other officers said with a great big smile on his face.

I reached my hand out through the window and shook the officers' hands.

The officers shook my hand proudly as if they were shaking the hands of a superstar. The officers were grinning, smiling, and gawking at me.

"Louis, follow us into town," the officers said as they walked back to their motorcycles. They jumped back on their motorcycles and sped up ahead of my truck. The officers motioned me to follow them.

I started my truck and followed the officers. I wondered exactly what they had up their sleeves with them wanting to escort me into my hometown.

As I was about to enter the Griswold town limits I wondered, *How did they know I was driving back to town today? Why are they treating me like a star? What kind of surprise do the officers have for me?* My mind was burning with curiosity.

The police officers on motorcycles led me into what appeared to be a hometown parade. There was a giant banner stretched across the width of Main Street and was tied to buildings on each side of the street. It read WELCOME HOME LOUIS! in large bold red print. There were crowds of people lined up on both sides of the street. They were cheering, clapping, shouting, and waving American flags as the police officers escorted me slowly through the crowd. It was a chilly December day in Griswold, and it was amazing to see all of those people lining the streets bundled up in their coats.

I waved to as many friends as I could. My heart was overwhelmed with excitement and deep emotion. Nothing in my life had ever moved me quite like this. Tears streamed down my face. *Are all of these people here for me? Do I really have all of these friends? How did they know the precise day and time that I was returning to town?* These questions continued to puzzle me.

"Go Louis!" the crowd shouted. "Our hero, our hero!"

As I continued to pass the crowd, I noticed a whole team of news reporters had lined the streets. There was the local television station crew, ABC, NBC, CBS, FOX, and CNN all there to cover the event. I was humbled by their presence, but at the same time I was annoyed that the press was there. I dreaded the thought of having to face a whole new round of questions being lobbed at me about the bank robbery-hostage incident that happened only a few days ago.

How could they still be interested in a story that happened that long ago?

As I continued to drive down Main Street I noticed an overflow crowd of people. There were only 1,000 or more people who lived in the town, but there appeared to be a crowd of well over 10,000.

Man, word travels fast. How could there be so many people?

The parade continued to move slowly through town and passed the funeral home and water tower. Suddenly the parade

The Contrary

came to a crawl. The officers stopped their motorcycles in front of the Griswold Community Center. The crowds rushed over to see what all the commotion was about. The officers motioned for me to park my truck. About eight police officers surrounded my truck to keep the crowd at bay. The officers opened my door and helped me out. They completely surrounded me like the Secret Service does for presidents. They helped me move slowly and carefully through the sea of people trying to talk to me and touch my hands. There were photographers, news reporters, and autograph-seekers all swarming on me as if I were some kind of world celebrity figure.

The officers pulled on my arms trying to maneuver me into the community center. Sometimes they lifted me off of the ground. Sometimes it felt like they were dragging me. I was overwhelmed by the large enthusiastic crowd cheering and chanting for me. I felt like a football superstar who had just won the Super Bowl and was being showered by all his fans.

Finally the officers were able to lead me into the community center. Inside the center were large banners draped in red, white, and blue. The center was colorfully decorated. The banners read WELCOME HOME LOUIS! There were chairs and bleachers set up for the crowds as they poured into the center.

The officers led me to a stage, which was positioned in the center of the community center. A middle-aged handsome man over six feet in height walked up to give me a hug. I immediately recognized the familiar face.

"Hi Jerry," I shouted enthusiastically over the noise of the crowd.

"Welcome home, Louis. We are so proud of you."

Most of the citizens of Griswold referred to the mayor as Jerry instead of Mayor Bradley.

"I will be introducing you. We would love to hear from you and what you have to say," the mayor said enthusiastically.

I gulped for air and swallowed deeply.

Suddenly I felt dizzy and sick to my stomach. *How did I get into this mess? Do I really have to speak to this crowd?*

I felt weak in my knees at the sight of the large standing-room-only crowd that had suddenly appeared in the community center.

The Griswold High School Band played the National Anthem as everyone rose to their feet to salute the large American flag hanging from the ceiling.

After the band stopped playing, there was a thunderous applause. Mayor Jerry Bradley stepped forward to the podium to say a few words. He adjusted the microphone so that he could be heard.

The noisy crowd became silent.

"This is a proud and joyous moment, a special day we will always remember here in Griswold. We salute our hero Louis Green for the brave and heroic act he performed on Monday in Omaha," the mayor boasted.

Almost immediately, thunderous cheering and applause erupted.

I sat in my chair on stage swirling in a sea of nervousness and wondering what I was going to tell the crowd.

"Louis Green saved those police officers and the security guard in that bank. He apprehended those dangerous masked men who held up the bank and held those people hostages—what a hero."

The crowd responded with overwhelming excitement as they cheered and applauded over and over again.

It took a while to calm the crowd so that the mayor could speak again.

"Now I present to you our hometown hero Louis Green," the mayor shouted loudly and proudly. The crowd erupted in thunderous applause, cheering as the band played a rousing rendition of a John Sousa March.

My mind started to drift as I looked around the overfilled

The Contrary

crowd of people chanting, cheering, and applauding. It felt like the applause lasted almost ten minutes. I felt intoxicated from the excitement of the crowd. It was a long, warm, and heartfelt greeting. I felt sick and needed some fresh air. The air in the community center had become stale from all of the people packed into the building.

I finally pulled myself together. I took a deep breath and stood out of my chair. I walked slowly to the podium and adjusted the microphone.

Louis, you can do this.

Before I said a word, I looked around the entire community center as if I was searching for a long lost friend. It must have been at least 20 seconds before I said a word. The crowd grew still and patient waiting to hear something from their *superstar hero*.

I felt self-conscious as I noticed the entire front row of television cameras pointed at me. My mind drifted back to reality as I pulled myself together.

"It is humbling and overwhelming to see such a turnout. And it is humbling to be called a hero. But I really don't feel like I deserve to be called a hero," I said as I broke down with tears.

The crowd remained silent.

"For so long I have treated my family and my friends with contempt. I have been a despicable, judgmental, self-righteous, and bitter man," I tearfully confessed to the crowd.

The crowd remained quiet and listened to what I had to say.

"When I lost the love of my life Samantha to a long battle with cancer, I grew angry at God. I blamed God for everything. I started taking my anger out on my family and friends. Next thing you know, I was spouting off at the mouth to them about what I believed and forcing my opinions on others as if my opinion was the only right one. I am truly sorry to all of you for treating you that way."

"We love you, Louis," a man shouted in the crowd.

"You are our hero," a woman shouted.

"Go Louis, go Louis," the crowd shouted as they suddenly broke out into a continuous chant.

I paused, smiled through my tears, and reveled in the glory. I looked around at the sea of chanting people, and it was overwhelming. I took another look, and I nearly stopped in my tracks. What I saw was frightening.

Oh, no. It's her again. She's following me around.

To the right of me in the far corner standing next to the exit sign was the same angelic woman figure that had appeared to me in the cemetery after my sister's funeral.

I started to tremble with fear. I looked away. Then I looked again and there she was, but this time she was shaking her head frowning with disapproval. I was scared stricken with panic.

Maybe something bad is about to happen. I might have a massive heart attack or the building might catch on fire. I could be in grave danger.

Then I pulled myself together so I could finish my speech to the crowd. I turned away from the angelic woman figure standing in the very back of the building and pretended that she didn't exist. I was not going to let some angel ruin my fifteen minutes in the spotlight.

The crowd became quiet as I began to speak again.

"I feel like I'm a changed man for the best since you last saw me. So much has happened so fast in the past week when I was in Omaha. First my sister Hilda fell to the floor fighting for her life and choking during our family Thanksgiving dinner. My daughter-in-law tried to save her by performing CPR. She was rushed to the hospital, and we waited for over 14 hours to hear some news on her condition. When we found out that she was in critical condition, we continued to pray for her. But we were so exhausted that we left the hospital to get some sleep at my son and daughter-in-law's house. Next thing you know, we found their house totally ransacked and robbed with obscenities smeared all over the wall in human excrement. Their favorite cat was murdered in cold blood. It was dreadful. We left their house after the police officers filed a report. We checked into a hotel and later that afternoon got a call from Hilda's husband that she went to be with Jesus in Heaven. The next day we got a call from the police station in Omaha saying they caught the sick person who ransacked and robbed our home. It turned out to be my nephew who was caught for those crimes. And then on Monday just before my sister's funeral, I ended up being held hostage in a bank robbery at the Bank of Omaha."

Before I could finish, a loud shot rang through the community center. I fell to the stage floor. A mysterious bullet had hit Mayor Bradley in the arm. The police officers immediately surrounded the mayor and me. The crowd went ballistic. There was panic everywhere. People were screaming and running in all directions to escape whatever had just happened.

"We need officer backup immediately to the community center. Some people have been shot," one of the officers shouted into his portable handheld radio.

The police officers drew their weapons as they held the mayor and me down, shielding us and trying to protect us from danger.

"Are you hurt?" one of the officers asked the mayor.

"I've been hit in the arm," the mayor shouted with a painful sounding voice.

"How about you, Louis, are you hurt?"

"I think I'm okay. My ear hurts a little bit," I replied as I lay on the floor trembling with fear.

One of the officers noticed that my right ear had been grazed apparently from the same bullet that had hit the mayor's arm. The officer made a tourniquet from his wide belt and wrapped it around the mayor's arm to keep him from bleeding. The crowd rushed to the nearest exits as pandemonium set in.

Backup officers including the Iowa State Police and the paramedics arrived on the scene. The paramedics rushed to the stage to deliver emergency treatment to the mayor and me. Some paramedics placed the mayor on a stretcher and carried him carefully to the ambulance with backup police officers protecting him. There were police officers everywhere in the building trying to get the crowd under control. Some of the officers had K-9 dogs with them and assault weapons. They were taking no chances. This could have been a terrorist attack, small town or not.

"There was a man near the exit sign with a gun," a woman in the crowd shouted to an officer.

"Which way did he go?" the officer asked as he rushed out the exit door in pursuit of him.

The news reporters and cameras from the major networks were swarming around the police officers and me, who were still on stage.

"Are you hurt, Louis?" one reporter asked as she tried to reach me, as I was surrounded by police officers.

"There has been a possible terrorist attack against the town of Griswold, Iowa," one reporter broke into the television audience on CNN News with the breaking story.

"Pandemonium is swirling everywhere in this crowd as Mayor Bradley of Griswold, Iowa, has been shot and Louis Green of Griswold has been injured," an ABC news reporter broke into the daily scheduled programming events to report this as breaking news.

"Mayor Bradley and Louis Green of Griswold, Iowa have been shot by what was described as a lone gunman during the hometown celebration held today for America's Hero Louis Green. The overflow crowd became panic stricken by the gunshot that rang out," the Fox News reporter repeated the breaking news story.

As the police officers cleared everyone out of the building, the police officers on stage surrounded me as they escorted me off stage and whisked me away in a police car to safety.

I sat in the back of the police car and tried to catch my breath after the pandemonium and confusion. I looked through the backseat window as the police car pulled out through the crowd. A large crowd had completely surrounded the car where I was sitting. Photographers, autograph-seekers, gawkers, and television cameras tried to force their way through the crowd to reach me. But the police car worked its way slowly through the crowd until it was finally free. As the police car drove down Main Street and headed to the police station, a million things ran through my mind.

I am lucky to be alive. I could have been killed if that bullet had come just a little closer. Was that bullet meant for the mayor or was it meant for me?

Cold shivers ran all through my body as I thought, *What if that bullet was meant for me? Who would want to kill me?*

Fear captured my mind and body. I trembled at the thought of someone wanting to kill me. I feared for my life.

Could that attempted murder incident back there in the community center have had anything to do with the angelic appearance inside the center moments before the gun went off?

Fear paralyzed me as I remained quiet and my body trembled in the back seat of the police car. There was a stalker killer on the loose and that killer could be looking for me. Time would tell. I didn't have much time left.

CHAPTER TWENTY-THREE

INVITATIONS GALORE

After I was transported to the police station and questioned about the earlier attempted murder incident of the mayor and me at the community center, I was escorted to my farm located on the other side of Griswold.

"We'll set up 24-hour police protection for you, Louis," Officer Jones assured me. "We'll get your truck and bring it to you. If you need to leave your house for anything, we promise to protect you."

"Thank you, Officer Jones. That makes me feel safer and more at ease, especially with a killer out there running loose trying to hunt me down."

Night started to fall early since it was December with some of the shortest days of the year. Officer Jones shook my hand as he closed the front door behind me and walked down the front porch steps toward his police car. He was the first officer to take the night shift as he sat outside my farmhouse on the dirt driveway watching and waiting for any suspicious activity.

I kicked back in my easy chair and decided to catch some of the news on my big screen television before bedtime. I kept watch out of the side of my eyes and never took one eye off the police car parked outside in my front driveway.

I surfed through the news channels and suddenly caught a glimpse of myself on CNN News. There was the pandemonium of today's hometown hero event at the Griswold Community Center being played for the whole world to see. CNN showed video clips of the mayor speaking, then clips of me speaking. The clips of the mayor and me lying wounded on the stage floor followed. You could see the crowd filled with hysteria running in all directions after the gunshots were fired. There was a video clip of the mayor being carried off on a stretcher by the EMS in an ambulance, and there was one clip of me being whisked away in a police car. The caption GRISWOLD MAYOR JERRY BRADLEY AND HOMETOWN HERO LOUIS GREEN SHOT AT WELCOME CELEBRATION flashed across the screen.

As I watched those videos playing over and over on CNN, FOX, ABC, NBC, and CBS, I thought, *If they didn't know who I was before today, I'm sure now everyone will know my name.*

The phone rang and I answered it.

"Dad, this is Norris. I am calling because I'm worried about you. You're all over the news. Are you okay?"

"Yes, Son, I'm okay. What happened today was awful. I feel lucky to be alive. I could've been killed by the bullet that hit the mayor. But what matters most is that there is a crazy psychopathic killer out there running loose. I think he is trying to kill me. The Griswold Police have offered 24-hour protection for me. In fact, right now there is a police officer watching for any danger outside my house."

"Seriously?"

"Yes, for real. And to tell you the truth, I'm scared out of my wits to step foot out of this house knowing that I could be lying in a coffin tomorrow."

"What can I do for you, Dad? Do you need me to come down there and stay with you?"

"No, not right now, but thanks for offering."

"Well, Dad, I'll be thinking about you and will check on you frequently."

I hung up the phone, but before I could sit in my easy chair, the phone rang again.

I picked up the phone and answered, "Son, I'll be okay, don't worry."

I heard an unfamiliar voice that sounded scrambled with some kind of electronic mechanism to make the voice unrecognizable.

"You better watch every step you take," the voice warned. "I'm going to find you, hunt you down like a deer, and kill you. I'm going to watch you suffer. Watch you take your last breath as you lie in your own pool of blood."

I continued to listen to the voice on the other end of the phone.

"I missed last time. But next time, I won't miss."

"Who is this?" I asked with fear in my voice.

I could hear heavy breathing on the other end. Then there was silence. The caller with the strange voice had hung up.

Fear struck my entire body. I felt shivers of terror running through my body. Now I realized with certainty that I was the target of the killer.

Who would threaten my life? What motive would someone have to want to kill me? Does the angelic figure have anything to do with this death threat?

Sure I had been a despicable, judgmental, ruthless, and opinionated man in the past, but I didn't believe anyone took me seriously enough to want to kill me.

I picked up the phone and called my son again.

"Son, this is Dad," I said with a shaking voice.

"What's wrong, Dad?"

"I just got a threatening phone call a few minutes ago from a stranger who said he was going to kill me."

"Seriously?"

"Yes, Son, as serious as a heart attack. He claimed responsibility for today's attack at the community center. He said that he missed, but that next time he wouldn't miss and would kill me. He described how he would kill me, and said he would find me and hunt me down like a deer. I'm scared, Son. He had a strange voice that sounded like it was manipulated by an electronic device to disguise his identity."

"Did you call the police?"

"No, not yet. You were the first person I called."

"Go ahead and call the police so that they can put a tracer on your phone lines next time he calls."

"I will. In fact when I hang up with you, I'm going to tell Officer Jones exactly what happened."

"Goodbye, Dad. I love you."

"Bye, Son. I love you so much."

After I hung up, I reached for my coat in the closet and opened my front door cautiously. It was so cold outside that I could see my breath before me in the moonlight. I walked down the front porch steps and approached Officer Jones's car. I tapped on the window loudly. Officer Jones rolled down his window.

"How can I help you?"

"Can I talk to you?" I asked with an anxious sounding voice.

"I unlocked the door. Come around to the front passenger side and let's talk."

I opened the front passenger side door, stepped inside the police car, and shut the door.

"Okay, Louis, talk to me."

"After I hung up the phone with my son Norris, I got a threatening call from this man. His voice sounded very strange as if it were being altered by some kind of electronic device."

"Well, what did he say?"

"He told me that he missed today at the community center

event. He said that next time he wouldn't miss. He told me that he would find me, hunt me down like a deer, and kill me in my own blood. I asked him who he was and then he hung up," I said with a fear-stricken voice. "Now I know that I am the target of this killer."

"That bastard, he won't get away with this. We will find him. I am requesting that we put a tracer on your home phone line so that the next time he calls to threaten you, we can track him down," Officer Jones tried to reassure me.

"Meanwhile, what should I do?"

"I would just stay put. Lock your doors. Don't answer the door for any reason. We are here 24/7 to protect you."

"Okay, thanks Officer Jones," I shook the officer's hand and opened the car door to walk back to my house.

I opened the front door of my house and locked it with the dead bolt. I made a complete inspection of every door and window to make sure they were bolted down securely. I left the light on in the downstairs living room and walked upstairs to my bedroom.

I brushed my teeth, washed my face, and put on some clean pajamas. I pulled out the top dresser drawer in my bedroom and picked up my .38 revolver. I checked to make sure that the gun was loaded. I turned my night light on, turned my bedroom lights off, and tucked myself into my warm, cozy bed. I laid my gun right beside me in case there were any intruders during the night. I said a prayer to God begging Him for mercy and protection and asked Him to help the police find the killer before the killer found me. I was exhausted and soon fell asleep.

The next morning, the sun shone brightly through my upstairs bedroom window and woke me. I stretched my arms and legs and looked around. There were no angels and there had been no night intruders. I thanked God for sparing me for another day.

The clock in my bedroom flashed 10:05 a.m. I had slept for

more than 10 hours. I rolled over and jumped out of bed. I put my feet into my warm fleece-lined bedroom slippers, picked up my gun, and tiptoed downstairs toward the kitchen. On my way to the kitchen, I peeked out from behind the drapes and blinds of my front living room window. I noticed that the police were still there as they had promised. That reassured me. The phone rang before I could get to the kitchen. Fear struck my body like a bolt of lightning.

Should I pick up the phone? Could it be the man with the strange voice who said he was going to kill me?

I hesitated for a moment as the phone continued to ring. I decided to pick it up.

"Is this Louis Green?"

"Who is this?"

"This is Arnie Tidwell with *The After Hours Show* on NBC."

"Seriously?"

"Yes, for real."

"I love that show. I watch it almost every night before I go to bed," I said excitedly.

"I'm glad you love the show. I'm the talent coordinator, and we would love to have you as our guest."

"Well, how did you hear about me?"

"Ha, ha, you're kidding me, right?"

"I kid you not."

"Everyone knows your name Louis after what happened with the Bank of Omaha bank robbery-hostage incident and what happened yesterday when you and the mayor were almost killed. You are *America's Hero*," Mr. Tidwell said raising his voice with excitement.

"Wow, I had no idea," I pondered what Mr. Tidwell had just said. "So you want me to be a guest on the show?"

"Yes, most definitely. In fact, Mr. Callahan asked me to personally call you to invite you on the show."

"The Chris Callahan? No way. Get out of here."

"Oh, yes. He's a big fan of yours."

"Wow, well I'm honored to have been asked. Could you please give me 48 hours to check my schedule and get back with you?"

I can't tell him that a stalker is trying to kill me and that I am too scared to go on his show for fear of being murdered.

"Could you call me by 2 p.m. tomorrow? Here's my number 818-557-8989."

"Alright, I will."

As soon as I hung up the phone, I jumped up and down repeatedly with sheer excitement over being invited to appear on the *The After Hours Show.*

Yes, yes, yes, I chanted to myself.

I picked up my home phone and called my son.

The phone rang four times and then Norris answered.

"Son, you won't believe what happened to me a few minutes ago," I said with excitement in my voice.

"They caught the killer?"

"No, I'm afraid not."

There was a brief moment of silence.

"I got invited to be a guest on *The After Hours Show.*"

"That's awesome, Dad. Have you set a date for the show?"

"No, I told him I would get back with him in 48 hours. I'm not sure about whether I should make the trip to Los Angeles, when I don't know if it's safe or not for me to travel with this killer on the loose."

"You could ask the police to escort you to the airport and alert security at the airport to watch for any suspicious characters. Once you are in L.A. you should be fine. If I were you, I would do it. That is an opportunity of a lifetime. It's not every day that you get invited to be a guest on the *The After Hours Show* with Chris Callahan. Go for it, Dad."

"I think I just might do it."

I had been so preoccupied with the thought of being on *The*

After Hours Show and talking with my son that I forgot all about eating breakfast. It was time to eat lunch. The clock on the wall read 12:22 p.m. I grabbed my laptop computer and walked to the kitchen to fix myself a sandwich. I opened my computer, logged in, and opened my email inbox. To my amazement, my inbox was overflowing with messages from national and local newspaper reporters; morning, daytime and late night show hosts; and from news talk show hosts all requesting an interview or an appearance on their shows. It was overwhelming.

How can I ever find the time to answer all of these emails? If I accept these invitations now, I could put myself at risk to be killed by that stalker. If I were to accept every one of those invitations, I wouldn't be doing anything else except doing interviews and being a guest on all of these shows.

As I closed my inbox to put my computer away, the phone rang. I was going to make a sandwich. I decided to let my phone go to voice mail as I felt totally overwhelmed and distracted by all the people wanting to interview me. I grabbed some bread from the counter and fixed myself a turkey sandwich. I found some chips in the pantry and poured myself some ice tea.

The phone continued to ring over and over again. It was unbelievable how popular I had grown. I tried to capture a moment of silence, so I could regain my composure. As I was eating, I pondered the pros and cons of flying to Los Angeles to appear on my favorite show. I came to a conclusion that I didn't care if I ever did another interview in my lifetime, but I would at least do an interview with my favorite show host.

How bad could it be? If the police follow me to the airport and airport security is alerted, I should be safe.

I was excited about my decision to appear on my favorite show. Before I could finish eating my sandwich and chips, I picked up the phone and called Mr. Tidwell.

"The After Hours Show," a friendly female voice said.

"Yes, may I please speak to Mr. Tidwell?"

"May I ask who is calling?"

"This is Louis Green in Griswold, Iowa."

"Could you hold just a moment?"

There was silence on the other end. Then that familiar voice spoke.

"That was quick, Louis," Mr. Tidwell said.

"Yes, it didn't take me long to decide. I would be honored to be a guest on the show."

"That is great news. How about being on Monday night's show?"

"Monday night's show? Wow, that is fast. I thought you would have been booked for months."

"We are booked for months, but we had this last-minute opening for Monday, and we couldn't wait to have you on the show. You are *America's Hero* and the world wants to get to know you. We will book your flight for Monday morning leaving Omaha at 11:30 a.m. arriving at the LAX airport at 2:30 p.m. We will have a taxi waiting for you at the airport to take you to the studios."

"How will I know which cab to take?"

"There will be a man standing in the airport as you exit your plane. He will be carrying a sign with your name on it. Oh, and we will be filming the show at 4 p.m. that day. The show will actually air at 10:30 p.m. your time that evening, so tell your friends and family to watch. I will have a ticket waiting for you at the airport. Be careful and have a safe flight. I look forward to meeting you, Louis."

"Thank you, Mr. Tidwell. I can't wait to be on the show."

I was excited about the thought of being on the *The After Hours Show* with Chris Callahan. Finally it was becoming a reality. I had a lot to do to get ready for my flight to Los Angeles.

The Contrary

That would mean I would have to wake up early on Monday morning and leave Griswold at 7:30 a.m. so that I could be at the Omaha airport two hours early.

I spent the rest of the day packing and preparing for what I would say on the show. The threatening call I had received yesterday seemed like a distant memory. I paid it no mind. I had bigger and better things going on. I was going to be a guest on my favorite show on Monday night.

I'll be in Los Angeles. I'll be safe. No killer's going to bother me.

I turned the lights off so I could fall sleep. Little did I know the evil forces of darkness were lining up to take me down just as I was becoming comfortable and letting my guard down.

CHAPTER TWENTY-FOUR

A KILLER AT LARGE

I was in a deep sleep dreaming about my appearance on *The After Hours Show*. It all seemed so real. A loud repeated ring from my cell phone beside my bed woke me up. The clock read 10:01 a.m.

Who would be calling me? No one knows my cell phone number except my son and a few family members.

The phone continued to ring as if it were an urgent call.

"Hello."

I was so drowsy that it was difficult for me to comprehend much of anything.

"Did you miss me?"

"Who is this?"

"Did you see my picture on the news? Don't you think I'm handsome?"

"Who is this?"

"You mean to tell me you haven't been watching the news? You sure are missing a lot. I'm all over the news on every channel."

"Who the hell is this?"

The Contrary

"I am free now. I am free to take you down and make you suffer in your own blood. I'm going to kill you. I'm going to enjoy it, and no one's going to stop me."

"You sick bastard. You'll never get away with this."

"I know where you live. I know every move you make, and I know where to find you," the strange voice said as he laughed with a twisted sick mind.

Before I could say another word, the stranger hung up.

I lay there in my bed in a state of shock.

That sick bastard, what a way to ruin someone's day, particularly on a Friday. Now what am I going to do?

I rolled out of bed, grabbed my faithful .38 revolver, and ran downstairs to the front living room. I cautiously peeked out of the blinds and drapes of the front window. There were now three Griswold police cars, the sheriff's car, and two Iowa State Trooper vehicles parked in front of my house. They were positioned in such a way as to barricade my driveway. There was something else that I hadn't seen before since the attempted murder calamity inside the Griswold Community Center. It appeared that I was attracting a lot of attention to the small town of Griswold. There were at least two lines of reporters and television camera crews perched outside my window behind the police cars. It looked like they had camped out and were ready to leap onto me like a pack of hungry lions.

Wow, I'm never going to be able to leave my house without the chance of getting killed or hounded by the press.

I shook my head in disbelief. I walked away from the front window and sat in my easy chair feeling overwhelmed. I turned on my television and surfed the news channels. A breaking news story on CNN News caught my eye.

"CNN News has just learned that 29 year old T. Bone Jones has escaped from the Nebraska State Penitentiary in Lincoln. He is armed and very dangerous. If you see him or have any information about his whereabouts, call the Crime Hotline at 1-

888-223-TIPS," the female news anchor said. A photograph of T. Bone Jones flashed on the screen.

I switched channels and watched the story on FOX News.

"Fox News has learned that T. Bone Jones one of the infamous masked men who was apprehended in Monday's Bank of Omaha hostage-bank robbery incident has escaped from the Nebraska State Penitentiary in Lincoln. One guard and one inmate have been killed in what appears to be a planned escape. T. Bone Jones is armed and dangerous."

I continued surfing news channels. There was a breaking news story on MSNBC News.

"Federal and state authorities are continuing their search for the missing fugitive T. Bone Jones who escaped from the Nebraska State Penitentiary in Lincoln Wednesday night. He is armed and dangerous. Apparently he had planned an escape when a delivery was made to the prison on Wednesday evening. T. Bone Jones is at large, and we urge everyone to take severe caution."

I had seen enough.

Could T. Bone Jones be the one who had been calling and threatening to kill me? If that is T. Bone Jones who called me, it means he is still in Griswold hiding out after he tried to kill me.

I became deeply alarmed at the possibility of what could happen to me in the near future.

I called my son.

"Dad, what's wrong?" Norris asked as he answered the phone.

"Have you seen the news? Something awful has happened."

"I've been too busy with work. I haven't seen the news."

"One of the masked men who held me hostage and robbed the Bank of Omaha escaped from the state prison in Lincoln on Wednesday."

"Oh, no…"

"Oh, yes. His name is T. Bone Jones. His mug shot is all over cable and network news. He killed a guard and an inmate during his escape. They say he's armed and dangerous."

Norris took a deep breath and sighed as if he was worried.

"What are you going to do, Dad?"

"I'm going to be very careful. He's hiding out here in Griswold waiting for the right time to kill me."

"Do you need me to come to Griswold and stay with you for a while?"

"Son, I'd love that but I am leaving for L.A. in less than 60 hours. I will be taping *The After Hours Show* with Chris Callahan. There are now six police cars parked outside my front window guarding the place. To make matters worse, there are at least 50 news reporters and television camera crew members camped outside my window waiting for me to walk out my front door."

"I'm sorry, Dad, about all the things you are going through. I can't ever remember so many terrible things happening to you or anyone in such a short period of time."

"That stranger who called on Thursday evening threatening me called again this morning bragging about his picture being aired all over the news networks. That surely must be T. Bone Jones who is threatening to kill me."

"Have you told the police about the latest episode?"

"No, I haven't, but I will when I hang up the phone with you. I love you, Son."

"I love you, Dad. Be careful and be safe. If you need me for anything, don't hesitate to call."

I hung up the phone.

It would be too chaotic to just walk right out the front door and tell Officer Jones about my last episode with the stranger who threatened my life.

I remembered that Officer Jones had given me his cell phone number in the event of an emergency. The number was stored in my cell phone directory. I found the number and called him immediately.

The phone rang several times.

"This is Officer Jones speaking."

"Officer Jones, this is Louis Green. I am hunkered down inside my house. I noticed that there is a large crowd outside, and I didn't want to create havoc by stepping out there."

"That's a wise choice, Louis. So what is on your mind?"

"This morning I got a call from that stranger who threatened to kill me. It was a little after 10 when he called. He was bragging about his picture being all over the network and cable news channels. He asked me if I had seen the news."

"I bet you're talking about the prison breakout at the Nebraska State Penitentiary in Lincoln, right?"

"Yes, that's the one."

"The Iowa State Police and the Griswold Police have been put on high alert in pursuit of T. Bone Jones. And he's no relation to me." Officer Jones tried to make light of the coincidence of their shared last name.

"Seriously though, we have reasonable cause to believe that T. Bone Jones may still be in Griswold. And it sounds like from the threatening calls you've been receiving, he's still trying to carry out his revenge against you, Louis."

"How frightening. He's not done with me yet."

"No, I'm afraid not Louis."

"I've also got another problem we need to talk about."

"What's that?"

"I've been invited to appear on *The After Hours Show* on Monday evening in L.A. The taping is at 4 p.m. L.A. time, and they are flying me out on Monday morning from the Omaha Airport."

"First, congratulations for that great news. I don't blame you for wanting to accept the invitation. I'm a huge fan of Chris Callahan, but this could be a big problem for us here at the police force.

The Contrary

We will need to escort you from your house to outside the town limits of Griswold. We will need the help of the Iowa State Police to escort you to the Nebraska State line. Then we will need the help of the Nebraska State Police to escort you all the way to the Omaha Airport to make sure you get on that plane safely, unless we catch that bastard first. It's going to take a coordinated effort to make this work. What time does your flight leave?"

"11:30 a.m."

"That means we will need to make sure that you leave your house safely by 7:30 a.m. Monday morning. Can you be ready by that time?"

"Yes, I will be ready by then."

"Okay, Louis, we are here to protect you. Just call me if anything else happens. We will do the same. We are going to put a tracer on your cell phone so that if that T. Bone guy calls again, we can trace it and get an idea of where in Griswold he might be."

"I'm not sure how he got my cell phone number."

"We aren't dealing with your average dumb criminal. This T. Bone guy has been in and out of prisons for years. He's smarter than you think. He's sneaky. He's going to be a tough one to catch. Get some rest, Louis, and take care of yourself."

"I will Officer Jones. Thank you for all you do."

"You're welcome."

I was growing weary from the stress and fear of the "unknowns" about the killer fugitive on the loose. I decided to relax in my easy chair. I held onto my revolver tightly and fell into my chair. I left my crazy *chaotic* world behind me and fell asleep.

While I slept, Officer Jones was making contingency plans with the other officers and the state troopers who were outside in front of my house guarding it.

"Gentlemen, this is the way it is. We've got a dangerous,

psychopathic killer on the loose trying to kill Louis Green. This fugitive T. Bone Jones could very well be right in front of our faces here in this town, and we may not even know it. He's smart and sneaky enough to distract us or throw us off track. So we need to anticipate all of his moves way ahead of what he is planning to do."

"What do you suggest we do?" one of the officers asked.

"We need to stay alert at all times and make sure no one slips past our barricade. That means that one of you officers needs to guard the back of his house, too."

"I'll do it." Officer Highland volunteered.

"Ok, great. Now we need to plan ahead for Monday. Louis will be leaving his house this Monday at 7:30 a.m. We will need to escort him from his house to a mile or so outside the town limits. The Iowa State Troopers will be taking over and will escort Louis to the Nebraska State line. From there, Louis will be escorted by the Nebraska State Police until they make sure that he is safely on the plane."

"Did I miss something? Where is Louis going?" Officer Highland asked.

"Oh, yes, I forgot to tell you the details. Sorry. Louis will be flying from Omaha to Los Angeles on Monday morning at 11:30 a.m. He will be taping an interview with Chris Callahan on NBC's *The After Hours Show*."

"That son of gun, wow, he's becoming really famous."

"Yes, we are very proud of Louis. They call him *America's Hero*."

The officers present agreed to the plan that they would implement on Monday morning. They returned to their guard duties while I slept.

I finally woke up at 8:06 p.m. I had dozed off in my easy chair and had forgotten to eat dinner. I also had forgotten to turn off my big screen television. I clutched my revolver and tiptoed to the front living room window. I carefully looked

The Contrary

outside. It was dark. All I could see were outlines of the officers' cars that were parked in front of my house and silhouettes of a crowd of people who were probably news reporters and television crew staff.

I felt as if I were trapped behind four prison walls. I could neither come nor go. True, I felt safe with the police officers watching over me, but I felt like a prisoner of my own making. I was sad that my *heroic* actions had come to this. I trembled with fear at the very thought of being brutally killed by T. Bone Jones. Little did I know that sooner than later, I would finally meet my fugitive stalker killer, and I would have to make some fast decisions. I was so exhausted that I fell asleep in my easy chair with my gun in my hand.

CHAPTER TWENTY-FIVE

READY FOR L.A.

All day Saturday and Sunday, I spent my time packing and preparing for my trip to California. I was so ready for Los Angeles. I couldn't wait to break free from all of what I was going through. Being cooped up in my house like a prisoner in a jail cell was no life at all. I was used to coming and going freely as I pleased without 24-hour police protection and without being hounded by the press.

I was done with television for a while. Every time I would turn on the news channels, all I would see was the tired, worn-out story about the escaped convict killer T. Bone Jones. There was speculation that T. Bone Jones was attempting to kill me in an act of revenge. The other story that ran over and over like a worn-out DVD was about the attempted murder of Griswold Mayor Bradley and me. That was old news to me. It happened days ago at the Griswold Community Center. Fame for me was exciting, but I had no idea it would cause me so much grief. I had become a prisoner partly because of fate and partly because of my heroic actions. But whatever the reason, I was beginning to dislike fame and all that went with it. Still, if I could appear as a guest on *The After Hours Show* that would be living the dream of getting to meet Chris Callahan.

All day Saturday and Sunday, the police were faithfully parked outside my house. The reporters and television news people were still camped there, too. They were reporting live from my farm trying to find any "breaking news" that they could dig up.

As I fell asleep Sunday night, I thought about how wonderful Los Angeles would be. I thought about how free I would be — free from all the chaos that had taken place in my small town of Griswold. I believed that since Los Angeles was such a large city, I could get lost in the city without anyone recognizing me or bothering me. I would soon discover how wrong I was.

CHAPTER TWENTY-SIX

THE MOTORCADE TO OMAHA

The alarm clock sounded with a piercing sound. It was 6:30 a.m. I turned over to go back to sleep but the alarm refused to let me. Finally, I shut the alarm off and stretched my arms and legs. I took several deep breaths, yawned, and got out of bed.

Today is the day I fly to L.A.

I realized I didn't have a lot of time before I would have to leave. I quickly showered, dried myself, and dressed into some summer clothes. The temperature outside in Griswold was 26 degrees, but I knew that the temperature in Los Angeles would be 72 degrees. I wore a blue-flowered Hawaiian shirt and light colored khaki pants with some shiny brown loafers. I grabbed my revolver and headed downstairs to the living room. I took a quick peek outside my front living room window. No, it wasn't a nightmare or a dream, the police cars and the news reporters were still parked outside waiting for me.

I fixed myself some quick breakfast of microwaved eggs and bacon with toast.

Before I could sit to enjoy my breakfast, my home phone rang.

The Contrary

It could be Norris or it could T. Bone Jones. Should I pick it up?

I decided not to pick up the phone and let the voice recorder retrieve a message.

"Did you think I'd forgotten about you?" the strange voice asked. "I've been watching you all weekend. I know where you're going and what you're going to do. You can't escape fate. I plan to kill you. Don't know when or where, but it will definitely happen. Kill you soon."

After hearing that voice mail message, I froze and was panic-stricken. I wasn't hungry and didn't eat the egg, bacon, and toast that I had made for myself. I picked up my cell phone and called Officer Jones.

"Louis, how are you. Are you ready to make the trip?"

"I just got this call from T. Bone Jones. It's all recorded. He claims he knows where I'm going and what I'm doing. He threatened me again. He said he was going to kill me."

"Don't worry, Louis, we're going to find him sooner than you think. And we're going to put him away behind bars for the rest of his life. Hold onto that recorded message. We will use that as evidence against him in court. Are you almost ready?"

"I'll be ready to go at 7:30 a.m. as we planned."

"Okay, call me on this phone just before you are ready to leave. I will walk to your front door and meet you inside."

"Okay, Officer."

I took a deep breath to relieve some stress. I sat in my easy chair in the living room clutching the pistol in my hands.

Am I a fool to leave my house and take this trip? What if I get killed trying to make it to Los Angeles? What if T. Bone Jones has something sneaky planned that we weren't expecting? Will the police be able to catch him before he kills me?

I prayed and meditated in silence asking the good Lord for mercy and protection as I traveled. Time quickly sailed by.

The clock in my living room read 7:28 a.m. I checked the time on my cell phone and it was accurate. I made the call on my phone as I was instructed to do.

"This is Officer Jones speaking."

"I'm ready."

"Okay, let's do it."

I grabbed my suitcase and set it by the front door. There was a loud knock at the door. I cautiously peeked through the tiny peephole to make sure it was Officer Jones. I unlatched the dead bolt lock and opened the door to let him in.

"Are you ready?"

"Ready as I'll ever be."

"Okay, I'm going to lock the front door and we are going to make a careful exit out the back door. When I count to three, we are going to quietly slip out the back door and walk through the woods behind your house. There are officers in the woods to protect you. There will be an unmarked police car waiting for you on the other side of the woods next to Barrel Creek Road."

While Officer Jones was instructing me inside my house, a CNN News reporter outside of my house broke a live news story.

"This is CNN News live coming to you from the farm of *America's Hero* Louis Green in Griswold, Iowa. We witnessed a Griswold Police officer with a suitcase entering the front door of the home of Louis Green at about 7:28 a.m. this morning. Louis Green has been held in his house since Thursday evening. We are waiting to see if Louis Green and Officer Jones will be exiting the front door shortly. This is CNN News live reporting to you."

"One, two, three," Officer Jones said as he and I quietly opened the back door of my house and tiptoed cautiously down the back steps of my deck. Officer Jones helped me with my suitcase, and we slipped into the wooded area behind my house without being seen.

The officers in the woods helped us step over thorn bushes and brush as we worked our way to Barrel Creek Road, which

The Contrary

was a small side road that lay parallel to my property. The police officers and I continued through the woods and had only a quarter of a mile left to go.

I was huffing and puffing trying to catch my breath.

"Come on, Louis, you can do it. We're almost there," Officer Jones tried to encourage me.

I was tired from the walk through the woods. It seemed like a five-mile hike to me. But I finally saw the unmarked police car by the side of the road.

"Here, Louis, let me help you get in the car," Officer Jones helped me into the back seat of the police car. He carefully placed my suitcase in the trunk.

The unmarked police car sped away and was joined by other police cars and state troopers, including two state troopers on motorcycles all to escort me through town. The officers had decided to take me through a back route, which bypassed the town. It was a route I hadn't taken in a long time, but I could still see the water tower from this side of town. As the car whisked me away, I looked back through the rear window and breathed a sigh of relief as I was finally leaving all the chaos behind.

The car passed a sign that read THANK YOU FOR VISITING GRISWOLD. As we entered highway 92, we were met by a fleet of eight Iowa State trooper cars and two officers on motorcycles. Officer Jones pulled his car over to the side of the road. He opened the door to help me out. He opened the trunk to hand me my suitcase.

An Iowa State trooper introduced himself.

"I'm Officer Hayes. You must be Louis Green. We'll take it from here," Officer Hayes helped me into his patrol car. He placed my suitcase in the trunk, and we sped away down highway 92 toward the Nebraska state line. It was a sight to see with the state trooper car being escorted by eight state trooper cars and two troopers on motorcycles through a straight line of nothing but cornfields on each side of the road. During the 35-minute drive, I remained quiet and didn't have anything to say to Officer Hayes. My mind drifted to Los Angeles. All I could think about was the sunny 70-degree weather, palm trees, and beaches.

I could see myself being interviewed by Chris Callahan in front of a live audience. It felt so good to daydream and let my mind wander.

The time passed quickly. As I drifted back to reality, I noticed we were entering the Council Bluff City limits.

"We'll be stopping to change cars after we cross the South Omaha Veterans Memorial Bridge," Officer Hayes said.

I didn't say a word. I listened. I stared out at the buildings and houses as we drove through Council Bluff, Iowa, and the last city before we crossed the state line. Minutes passed, and we were crossing the South Omaha Veterans Memorial Bridge. The Missouri River was beautiful in my eyes. The morning sun reflected off the water as I observed several barges moving slowly up the river. The sign at the end of the bridge said, WELCOME TO NEBRASKA. The state trooper's car slowly pulled over to a rest stop about a quarter of a mile on the Nebraska side of the bridge. The motorcade of police vehicles slowly pulled over to stop. Waiting ahead was a motorcade of Nebraska State Trooper vehicles and a few Omaha Police cars. Officer Hayes opened the back door of his vehicle and helped me out of the car. Several officers escorted me over to a Nebraska State Trooper vehicle. They hovered over me as if I were the President of the United States. Officer Hayes shook hands with Officer Beckham, who was responsible for transporting me to the Omaha Airport.

"Fine job, Officer Hayes," Officer Beckham praised Officer Hayes and the Iowa State Troopers for making it safely to the Nebraska State line without an incident.

"I will personally make sure that Louis Green makes it safely to the airport," Officer Beckham said as he helped me into the back seat of the trooper's car and packed my suitcase in the trunk.

The Nebraska State trooper cars pulled out onto highway 92 and started their short journey to the Omaha Airport better known as Eppley Airfield. There were eight Nebraska State trooper cars—four in front and four in back of the vehicle that I rode in. There were two Omaha Police leading the way on motorcycles at the front of the line. I felt like some *hot shot* from all of the attention I was receiving.

The Omaha skyline caught my eye as we merged onto the west bypass of 680. The motorcade continued to exit 61 and traveled west to 30th Street. The motorcycles led the way to Story Expressway, where we finally made our way to Abbott Drive South. My eyes opened wide as I stared at the Omaha Airport. I had never been to that airport, and it appeared large and sophisticated compared to the tiny hangers I knew.

The police motorcade pulled up to the departure gate of American Airlines. Officer Beckham was the first to get out of the vehicle. He opened the back seat car door and helped me out.

"It's 9:05 a.m. Omaha time. You have a little more than two hours before your flight leaves." Officer Beckham said to me.

One of the troopers helped me with my suitcase.

"Okay, Louis, when I say the words *field day* that means it is safe to enter the airport building. We will enter through the automatic double doors and walk straight to airport security. Is that clear?" Officer Beckham instructed me.

Five state troopers huddled around me to protect me. The other eight officers and troopers joined airport security in searching the airport area for any suspicious characters or activity. There were security guards with dogs who went ahead of the team of troopers. I remained next to the state trooper vehicle awaiting word that the area had been cleared and was safe to enter the building. Several troopers walked out of the building and spoke with Officer Beckham.

"Field day," Officer Beckham said as he and the trooper led me through the automatic double doors and straight to airport security.

The troopers escorted me through the airport terminal and we made our way through the airport security where I had my identification checked. My suitcase and I were scanned. Large crowds gathered around the security area. They stopped and stared at me being escorted by eight state troopers, four police officers, and four airport security guards with M16 automatic weapons and dogs. After the team of officers cleared security, they escorted me to gate C16 in the terminal where my jet would be departing.

Passengers waiting to depart crowded around the spectacle of me seated in the waiting area completely surrounded by a circular wall of police officers, troopers, and airport security guards.

"Would you like us to get you something to eat or drink?" Officer Beckham asked me as I waited patiently for my plane to arrive.

"Yes, some bottled water would be nice."

Officer Beckham sent an officer to a vendor food stand to purchase a bottle of water for me.

"Thanks, Officer Beckham."

"So I heard you're going to be interviewed by Chris Callahan on *The After Hours Show.*"

"Yes, I am."

"You're making quite a name for yourself, Louis."

"You can say that again. I can't go anywhere or do anything without being noticed. I hope it will be different in L.A."

"Yeah, well maybe that will be the case since L.A. is such a large city."

The time seemed to race by. The American Airlines

The Contrary

representative reached for the microphone beside her and requested that the passengers traveling to Los Angeles line up to board. I could see the Boeing 757 outside the large panoramic window. I was escorted onto the plane first by the officers and troopers. The other passengers waiting to board the plane stared at me being herded on by the officers. The officers and I walked down the long ramp that connected the terminal to the plane. The officers led me to the first class seat of row 3A.

"You should be good to go from here," Officer Beckham told me. "When you return to Omaha, we will repeat the same security drill that we did today except in reverse so that we can guarantee you will arrive safely to Griswold."

"Thank you for all that you have done for me. Thank you for making me feel safe."

"We are here to protect and serve."

I was unaware that the minute I set foot on that airplane, I was in grave danger with no one to protect me.

CHAPTER TWENTY-SEVEN

TRAPPED IN MID-AIR

After the officers, troopers, and airport security left the plane, the passengers boarded until every seat had been filled. The airplane door shut securely and the Boeing 757 started to back up from the terminal. The airline attendants recited their security drills as the plane taxied down the strip toward the runway. The plane stopped for a moment to wait for clearance. When it was cleared for takeoff, the Boeing 757 sped down the runaway as the plane lifted off the ground. The plane lifted higher and higher until it had reached a safe altitude for us to turn on our electronic devices and to walk around if needed. I decided to lean my seat back and take a nap. I rested my head against the side of the seat and dozed off.

I had been sleeping on the plane for over two hours when I was awoken from a strong turbulence that rocked the plane back and forth. The captain spoke on the intercom.

"May I have your attention, this is your Captain speaking. We are moving into some severe thunderstorms, and we are trying to climb altitude to avoid them. Please fasten your seatbelts. We will be hitting some patches of strong wind, and it

The Contrary

may get rough for a while. We are flying over Nevada and should arrive in Los Angeles in about 35 minutes."

About ten minutes later, the seat belt sign had turned off. The captain told us that it was safe to walk around. The choppiness of the turbulent plane ride earlier had turned into a smooth, stress-free ride.

I felt my bladder calling me to the restroom. I unfastened my seatbelt and stepped out of my seat. Before I could reach the restroom my eyes nearly popped out of my head. I froze in my tracks and panic suddenly struck me. There standing only a few feet from me and guarding the restroom door was that same angelic woman figure who had revealed herself to me multiple times.

"You are in grave danger," the angel warned me. "The man who is trying to kill you is on this plane. He has changed his identity and doesn't look anything like his real self."

I remained frozen and listened attentively to what the angel had to say.

"Where is he?"

"He is sitting behind you in row 6A. He is going to kill you. You must lock yourself in this restroom until this plane has landed. Do not open the door for anyone."

Fear ran down my entire body. As crazy as the angel's warning seemed I could not ignore her. I opened the restroom door, climbed inside, and bolted the door shut. I started praying as my legs and feet trembled.

I heard the angel speaking to me from outside the restroom door.

"You only have 25 minutes until this plane lands. Stay in there and don't answer the door."

Minutes passed slowly as I felt uneasy from claustrophobia. I felt sick to my stomach as the air began to grow thin. I wanted to break free of the walls of that tiny restroom, but I knew it was too dangerous.

There was loud pounding of a fist on the restroom door. It continued for some time.

"Are you okay?" an attendant asked.

I remained quiet and didn't answer.

Outside the restroom door, I could hear the attendants gathering together and talking.

"A passenger said she saw a distraught man talking to himself just before he entered the bathroom," one of the attendants said.

"He's been in there a long time. I'm worried that he could be doing something dangerous to himself or to this plane," another attendant said nervously.

The captain radioed to the control tower in Los Angeles.

"This is Alpha One American 262 about 20 nautical miles away from landing at LAX. There is a man locked in the restroom that appears to be dangerous and a threat to this plane. Prepare for a possible attack on ground as we land soon."

"That's a roger, 262 we are alerting all ground security."

The flight attendants continued to pound their fists on the locked restroom door where I remained safe and secure.

"May I have your attention, please fasten your seat belts as we will be approaching the runway of LAX in a few minutes," the captain said on the intercom.

As the plane descended onto the runway, I could hear that angelic voice warning me.

"Louis, stay in there until everyone has left the plane."

The landing gear engaged and the plane gradually descended until the wheels touched the runway. I could feel the plane come to a complete stop.

The seat belt sign turned off, and the passengers started to leave the plane. I remained in the restroom until I could hear complete silence.

Outside, the plane was surrounded by the L.A. Police, TSA agents and airport security. After the last passenger left the plane, police officers and security stormed the plane carrying weapons of every sort. They pounded on the restroom door.

"This is the police. Open this door at once or we will break it down."

My body trembled with fear of being arrested by the officers for terrorism.

"It is safe to leave," the angelic voice instructed.

The pounding on the door continued.

"Alright, alright, I'm coming out. I slowly opened the door.

"Put your hands behind your head," an officer demanded as he pointed an M16 automatic rifle at me.

I raised my arms and placed my hands behind my head as the officers apprehended me. They handcuffed and paraded me off the airplane. There were at least a dozen police officers and security guards pointing weapons at me.

I slowly and carefully walked the airplane ramp toward the terminal. As the officers escorted me into the terminal, I noticed a suspicious looking man who fit the description of what the angel said was the *new identity* of T. Bone Jones. The man was staring at me. He smiled deviously, gave me the finger, and then aimed his finger at me like he was firing a gun.

The officers led me down the escalator stairs and we entered a door that read DO NOT ENTER: AUTHORIZED PERSONNEL ONLY. There was a long wooden table with a few chairs. The officers seated me at the table and stood around me.

A statuesque and muscular TSA agent by the name of Officer Tillis stood directly in front of me. He spoke with a deep, rough, and gravelly voice.

"What the hell just happened back there?" Officer Tillis asked me.

I didn't speak a word. I was afraid.

"I'm talking to you, son," Officer Tillis raised his voice.

After several minutes of interrogation, I finally bowed to the officer's request.

"I am not who you think I am," I replied meekly.

"Well then, why don't you tell us who you really are," the officer said as he paced the floor around me.

There was silence.

"I am Louis Green a retired factory supervisor. I live in Griswold, Iowa."

"State the nature of your business in Los Angeles," Officer Tillis replied.

"I have been invited to be a guest on *The After Hours Show.*"

"Louis Green? You're Louis Green from the bank robbery? Louis Green, America's Hero?" Officer Tillis asked.

"That's what they call me."

"So why did you lock yourself in the bathroom on the plane?"

"I was afraid."

"You're afraid of flying?"

"No, I'm afraid of being killed by a man who was sitting behind me."

"How do you know he was going to kill you?"

"He broke out of the Nebraska State Penitentiary last Wednesday and has been stalking and threatening me."

"Who is this scumbag?"

"They call him T. Bone Jones."

"T. Bone Jones, the convicted killer. Wasn't he one of the armed masked men who held you hostage in the Bank of Omaha about a week ago?"

"Yes, he's the one."

"We ran a thorough security check of all of the passengers on that plane, and no one fits his description or his name."

"He's changed his identity."

"How do you know that?"

"I just know."

"You mean you think you know or you actually know."

"I know."

The Contrary

If I tell them that an angel on the plane told me, they will surely lock me up, I thought to myself.

Officer Tillis was growing frustrated. He could see that he was wasting his time going around in circles with me, so he decided to unlock the handcuffs and let me go.

I walked out of the Homeland Security office and sprinted to the front terminal door. I had wasted nearly two hours with Homeland Security over the plane incident. I had missed the taxi driver who had been waiting to transport me to the NBC Studios. I motioned for a taxi to stop as I had only 40 minutes to arrive before the show began.

A taxi stopped and a guy with dreadlocks wearing a fedora helped me with my luggage.

"Where you going man?" he asked with a broken accent.

"Take me to the NBC Studios in Burbank. Please hurry. I've got a taping at 4:00 p.m."

"No problem."

The taxi driver knew I meant business. He did his best to get to the NBC studios as fast as he could. I took the time to reflect on what had happened on the plane earlier. I was excited to have been invited by my hero Chris Callahan to appear on his show, but the memory of T. Bone Jones standing in the airport a few hours ago aiming his finger at me like a gun still haunted me.

How did he know I was in L.A.? How did he slip past security?

Knowing that T. Bone Jones was in L. A. sent cold shivers down my body. I shuddered at the thought of what might happen next.

CHAPTER TWENTY-EIGHT

THE AFTER HOURS SHOW DEBUT

The time on my cell phone read 3:42 p.m. as my taxi pulled up to the guard's booth at the NBC Studios in Burbank. The guard checked Chris Callahan's guest list with my driver's license.

"You're in building 13A. Go straight and turn right where the sign says 13A."

The taxi driver took me to building 13A. The driver carried my suitcase to the front door.

"We made it just in time," I said as I threw the driver a tip.

"Thanks, dude, good luck. Tell Chris I said hi."

I rushed through the studio front door and into the lobby area. A security guard stopped me.

"Who are you here to see?"

"I'm supposed to meet Mr. Tidwell for the 4 p.m. taping of the *The After Hours Show*."

"ID please," the guard examined my driver's license.

The security guard called Mr. Tidwell on his two-way radio. I waited a few minutes for a response.

"Okay, Mr. Tidwell is expecting you. I'll take you to the dressing room."

I followed the guard down the long hallway.

"You're cutting it close," the guard said.

"You're telling me. I would've been here earlier but I was stopped and held by airport security."

"What did they hold you for?"

"It's a long story. All that matters is that I'm here."

"You're lucky that you're not the first one on the show."

Before I could enter the dressing room, Mr. Tidwell greeted me outside the door.

"You must be Louis Green. How are you?" Mr. Tidwell asked as he shook my hand.

"I could be better."

"Chris is excited to meet you. You've got quite a following. Mr. Callahan can't wait to hear your story."

"I can't wait to meet Mr. Callahan. I am a huge fan of his. I have watched his show for years."

"There's no need to hurry since you are the last guest on the show. They will put some makeup on you, and then we will wire you with a microphone. Wait in here."

I entered the plush dressing room and sat in a comfortable leather chair. I stared at the glitzy mirrors and the numerous lights framing the mirror.

So this is what showbiz is like.

The airport scene earlier with security whisking me away in handcuffs off the plane and being grilled by some TSA agents was more than I could take. And the memory of T. Bone Jones smiling and aiming his finger at me like a gun was too traumatic to handle on any day.

I enjoyed the silence sitting there in my dressing room. The time passed.

The door opened to the dressing room and three buxom women dressed in tee shirts, cut-off shorts and high heels strutted in. They were chewing and smacking their gum.

"We're here to put some color on your face sweetie and

make you look pretty."

"Sit back while we do you," another woman giggled.

I was fidgety in my chair feeling uncomfortable from all of the unwanted attention.

"Relax and enjoy, babe," one of the women said.

The trio of women were working me over, patting blush and painting makeup all over my face. They were detailed in every way.

"There you go, honey. You look good as new," one woman laughed with a high pitch shrill.

I didn't say a word. I sat there in a state of culture shock.

"The sound guy will be in here soon," another woman said as she ran her fingers through my hair.

"See you later, baby doll," the third woman said as she strutted out the door.

I took a look at my new makeup job in the mirrors.

Damn, this doesn't look a thing like me. What did those broads do to me?

I reached for some tissues and attempted to wipe off some of the makeup. It was now 4:35 p.m.

A portly looking man with a ponytail and mustache entered the dressing room. He wore a tee shirt, shorts, and flip flops.

"I'm here to wire you. Stand, hold your arms out, and relax."

I stood and held my arms like the man told me. He attached a tiny microphone onto the collar of my shirt and ran the cord down my back. He clipped a small black box to the back of my belt and plugged in the microphone cable running through my shirt.

"There you go. You are wired. We will sound check you before you go on the show. We will come get you before you go on."

I sat there in silence. I let my mind drift back to all of the chaos and trouble that happened earlier.

My thoughts were suddenly interrupted by a man who

opened the door.

"We're ready for you. It's showtime."

"Okay, I'm as ready as I'll ever be."

I followed the man through the hallway to the elevator, which opened to the second floor. We left the elevator and continued down a hallway that took us directly behind the studio set. From where I was standing, I could clearly see the audience. My eyes filled with stars as my heart fluttered. I felt sick to my stomach and weak in my knees. There on the set sitting only 20 feet away was Chris Callahan live and in person interviewing one of my favorite actresses, Meryl Streep. I couldn't believe I was standing on the set ready to make my debut on *The After Hours Show*. It was a dream of a lifetime.

"Okay, cell phones off. We will need to get a sound check in two minutes," the man said.

As I reached to turn off my cell phone, I noticed a text waiting for me. Curiosity overwhelmed me, but as I read the text, I almost fell apart. My body froze with deep fear. I was panic-stricken. I felt helpless, not knowing what to do.

That bastard's not giving up.

I read the text over several times.

It said, "Surprise. I'm in the audience. I'm gonna kill you after the show."

The sound man tapped me on the shoulder.

"Sound check, please. Say one, two, and three over and over."

I appeared distracted as I turned off my cell phone.

"One, two, three, two, one, three," I said.

"Perfect. Standby."

As I waited, I felt dizzy, confused, and sick to my stomach. I thought about the millions of people who would be watching me on television.

"Our next guest is from Griswold, Iowa. Everyone knows him as America's Hero for his bravery and courage. One week ago he apprehended five dangerously armed masked men and saved many lives in the Bank of Omaha bank robbery-hostage attempt. Please welcome Louis Green," Chris Callahan said as he stood to welcome me.

There was thunderous applause and cheering from the audience as everyone stood to salute me. The applause continued for over 10 seconds.

I was humbled by the warm and enthusiastic welcome. I took a seat across from Chris Callahan and smiled nervously.

"Thank you, thank you," I said as I continued smiling.

"It's so good to have you on the show. How are you?"

"I'm a little nervous and rattled because of what happened to me today. I was apprehended and placed in handcuffs by some TSA agents. And then I was grilled as to why I came here to L.A. I told them I was a guest on your show, and they let me go," I said as the audience burst out with laughter.

"Wow that was some L.A. welcome."

"You're telling me."

"So tell us about what happened last Monday in the Bank of Omaha robbery-hostage incident."

"I'm a huge fan of yours Mr. Callahan."

"Call me Chris. The feeling is mutual, Louis."

"So what happened in that Bank of Omaha robbery-hostage attempt last Monday?"

"Well, I was minding my own business, and I walked into the bank trying to cash my Social Security check. The teller had just counted out the bills and placed them in my hands. As I walked toward the front door to leave, five masked men stormed us with AK-47's and Uzi's yelling at everyone to fall to the floor. So I did what they told me to do," I said as I tried to catch my breath.

"What happened next?"

"They shot the security guard who was standing by the vault. A little later, four police officers stormed the building and

The Contrary

there was a standoff between the police and the masked men. It was a tense situation."

"How did you outsmart them?"

"Well, I can't take all of the credit. The police officers and two customers sadly ended up being shot to death. The Omaha Police and the SWAT team had the bank building surrounded. I felt completely helpless."

"I don't understand how you saved everyone and captured the masked men."

"Well, there was this angel who appeared out of nowhere."

"Was she hot? Was she a babe?" Chris asked as the audience roared with laughter.

"I have been reluctant to tell anyone about this angel knowing that probably no one would believe me."

"Seriously, you saw an angel with wings?"

"Yes, I most certainly did whether you believe me or not," I started to feel uncomfortable.

The audience became silent waiting for what I was about to tell them next.

"The angel came to my rescue. The armed masked men started firing many rounds of ammunition at the angel. The angel with some kind of extraterrestrial powers stripped them of their weapons. The masked men shook their fists and rushed the angel. They cursed her and tried to kill her, but she won."

"Wow, what a story. Is there more?"

"Yes. The strangest part came when the dead police officers, security guard, and customers opened their eyes and stood before the masked men. They literally resurrected before my eyes." The audience gasped with awe.

"That is quite a story."

"There's more. When all of those people woke up from the dead, the five masked men became very afraid. They knew they had riddled the bodies with bullets. They knew that it was impossible for dead bodies to come back to life. That is why it scared them so much. When the police and security guard were resurrected, they found their guns lying next to them. They grabbed their guns and pointed them at the masked men. The men surrendered, fell to their knees, and were handcuffed."

I could hear the audience reacting with sighs and gasps for breath as I shared my story.

"Thanks to that angel, the police officers, security guard, and I paraded the men outside of the bank as the SWAT team apprehended them."

Before I could say another word, the whole audience stood up applauding and wildly cheering me with a thunderous sound.

"Wow. That's an extraordinary story. What are your future plans?"

I paused in silence and stared into the audience. I appeared to be distracted and preoccupied.

"What's wrong?"

"There's a man in the audience who is trying to kill me," I whispered to Chris as I caught a glimpse of a bright light illuminating around an angelic figure standing in the back behind the audience.

The audience sighed with shock from what I had said.

"Are you sure a man is trying to kill you?" Chris asked as he tried to make light of it.

Chris tried to change the subject, so he could wrap up his interview with me.

"Thank you Louis for being a guest on my show. Let's give America's Hero one more round of applause," the audience stood to cheer and applaud me again.

The network cut to a commercial break. Chris shook my hand and thanked me for appearing on the show. I tried to put on my best smile despite the fact that I may have just looked like a *bonafide, certified kook* to America's audience who would watch the recorded show later that evening.

The Contrary

I shook the hands of the other guests. I felt awkward after talking about angels and a killer. As I walked toward the dressing room, the sound guy helped me remove the microphone that was attached to my shirt.

"That was terrific. The audience loved your story," Mr. Tidwell said to me.

"Thanks, Mr. Tidwell, for inviting me. I have a favor to ask of you. Is it possible for your security guard to walk me to my taxi outside of the studio?"

"Why sure, anything for you Louis."

Mr. Tidwell radioed for security. The security guard responded to Mr. Tidwell's request and introduced himself.

"I'm Doug Smith. I'll be happy to escort you to your taxi."

"Thank you. I would feel safer if you walked me out."

"What's wrong?" Mr. Smith asked as we walked down the long hallway toward the front door.

"I received this text. Someone said they were going to kill me after the show."

"It's probably just a prank."

"I don't think so."

"Well, I'm here to watch you get to your taxi safely."

The two of us walked out of the front door. We got into a motorized golf cart and drove to the front guard's booth at the gate.

"Dear God," I whispered under my breath as I read a text message on my phone.

"What's wrong?" Mr. Smith asked.

"I just got another text that says he's waiting for me."

"Who's waiting for you?"

"The crazy man who is trying to kill me."

"Don't worry Mr. Green I will watch out for any suspicious characters," Mr. Smith replied.

Mr. Smith escorted me to the outside of the gate by the street. I waved for a taxi. A bright yellow taxi pulled up to the curb. Before the driver could open the door, a strange shadow of a figure appeared out of nowhere, rushed Mr. Smith, and shot him in the face. Mr. Smith pulled his gun and tried to fire back but fell to the sidewalk.

Realizing what had happened, I ran as fast as I could to escape from the stranger with a gun. The stranger chased me. There was no time to catch a glimpse of the stranger's face. I turned left and ran down a dark alley hoping I could outrun the gunman. I ran for my life even though I was out of breath. I turned right into another dark alley, and then turned right into a narrow walkway between two tall buildings. The gunman was gaining ground. I was out of breath but had to do something fast or I was going to die. As I turned the corner of the narrow walkway I threw boxes, garbage containers and anything I could find into the path of the gunman to try to slow him down. There was a fire escape ladder hanging from an old building to the right of me. I reached to grab the ladder, trying to climb to safety. But my body was dangling from the ladder. The gunman finally caught up with me. I was in a state of panic and defenseless. He aimed his pistol and fired several bullets at me. One struck the side of my head. I felt like my head had exploded. I couldn't hold on to the ladder anymore. The pain was unbearable. I had the most excruciating headache I'd ever felt in my entire life. I felt blood gushing from my face. I was too weak. I fell to the ground.

"Touché, Louis. You're a dead man," the strange gunman laughed uncontrollably. He walked away as if nothing had happened leaving me lying in a pool of my own blood.

CHAPTER TWENTY-NINE

THE EPIPHANY

"So that's my story to the best of my recollection. Oh, and there's something else that happened. The very last thing I remember after being chased and shot by that strange gunman is falling to the ground," I told the nurses and assistants as they gathered around my hospital bed.

Some of them wondered if what I was telling them was a dream. Others thought there might be some truth to the lengthy story I had just told them. And if all of it was true, how could I have remembered those details so clearly. You see, I had only been awake for the last 24 hours. I had miraculously awakened from a long induced coma of 28 days.

- TO BE CONTINUED -

ABOUT THE AUTHOR

THORNTON CLINE has been honored with Songwriter of the Year twice in a row by the Tennessee Songwriters Association for his hit song, "Love is the Reason" recorded by Engelbert Humperdinck and Gloria Gaynor. He has received Dove and Grammy Award nominations for his songs. His articles have appeared in numerous national magazines and journals. The Contrary is Cline's sixth published book. He is author of Band of Angels, Practice Personalities: What's Your Type?, Practice Personalities for Adults, The Amazing Incredible Shrinking Violin and The Amazing Incredible Shrinking Piano. Cline is an in-demand speaker for national conferences and workshops. Cline lives in Hendersonville, Tennessee, with his wife and two children.

PREVIEW

THE CONTRARY: A TRAVESTY OF JUSTICE is the follow up novel to THE CONTRARY. Here is an excerpt from chapter one of the new soon-to-be released sequel.

JANUARY 18, 2010 5:12 P.M.
WEST OMAHA, NEBRASKA

The 911 call came from a frantic and distraught caller.

"911, what's your emergency?" the operator asked.

"I heard a loud gunshot. I think someone's been hurt or killed, I was walking the dog in the neighborhood, help, please help," the caller said as he rushed through his words.

"Slow down, stay calm and tell me the address," the operator commanded.

"I'm, I'm at 396 Seymour Lane," the caller said as he tried to catch his breath.

"Okay, emergency vehicles are on the way. Sir, stay calm and tell me your name."

"I'm Charles Talley. I live next door to the house where I heard the gun go off. I'm worried about my neighbor, Pastor Hershel. He's inside the house and could be seriously injured."

"Officers and emergency vehicles are on the way," the operator said.

"Are you alright Mr. Talley?"

"Yes, thank you but I'm worried about my neighbor. It's quiet now and the lights are on."

"Do you see anyone inside or anything suspicious?"

"No, not that I can tell."

"Ok, stay calm we are only a few blocks away."

Charles could hear the wailing of the sirens in the distance as they grew closer.

All at once, flashing blue lights appeared over the horizon of the street.

First, the police cars arrived, and then the ambulance and fire trucks all quickly pulled up to the curb of 396 Seymour Lane.

"Is this the house?" an officer asked.

"Yes," Charles replied.

The officers and paramedics rushed up the steps to the front door. The officers rang the doorbell and knocked on the door repeatedly. There was no answer.

"This is the police, open the door," the officers shouted.

There was no answer only silence. An officer jiggled the door handle.

"It's locked sir," an officer said to the others.

The officers drew their pistols as the others kicked the door down.

They rushed into the house pointing their weapons in all directions. The officers searched the living room, kitchen and dining room but found nothing.

They slowly climbed the stairs of the two-story house with their guns pointed ready to fire.

Once the officers reached the top of the stairs they turned and slowly walked the long hallway with their weapons pointed in all directions. They turned right and slowly opened the bedroom door.

As they entered the bedroom slowly their eyes opened wide with alarm and they took it all in. To the right of them beside the bed was a man slumped down against the wall soaked in a pool of blood. Beside his right hand was a .38 caliber pistol lying on the floor. To the left above the body were blood stains seeping down the wall still fresh from a crime that had occurred less than an hour ago. There were pieces of grey matter from the brains still intact on the wall and floor where he lay.

There was no sign of life. The paramedics were careful not to disturb the body. The police took photos and wrapped the bedroom with yellow tape which read, POLICE LINE: DO NOT CROSS."

- TO BE CONTINUED -

Purchase other Black Rose Writing titles at www.blackrosewriting.com/books
and use promo code PRINT to receive a 20% discount.

BLACK ROSE writing™